# THE RANCHER TAKES HIS STAR CROSSED LOVE

THE RANGERS OF PURPLE HEART RANCH BOOK 4

SHANAE JOHNSON

THOSE JOHNSON GIRLS

# CHAPTER ONE

"Rosalind just broke up with me."

David Porco flicked at the propeller of the drone at his feet. The rotor gave a buzzing whirl of sympathy at his pain. The whir was short-lived as the drone wasn't powered on. Without the engines in gear, the blades barely made a full rotation. Had the device been ignited, Porco was certain he'd get a more resounding response from the drone. He was barely getting a hum out of his friend.

"Didn't you tell me you were going to break up with her two days ago?" Jordan Spinelli's fingers picked over the fuses in the exposed belly of the drone's controller box. "Because you no longer felt *the spark.*"

Spinelli's last two words were said with a sneer of his lips and roll of his eyes. The man's mind was far too scientific to believe in the power of true love, or what Porco's mom called the spark. The flare of feeling across the spine and down to the fingertips. The rise in temperature that wasn't hotter than a fever, and at the same time cooled the entire body. That spark was what let her know that Porco's father had been the man of her dreams. His father had admitted to the feeling too.

Nelson Porco had told his son that the spark had been a racing of his heart. He'd heard his pulse pounding in his ears. His mouth had gone dry, but he'd drooled all the same when he'd caught sight of Hailey Baker, the woman who would just a few days later become his wife.

Porco had been chasing that feeling since he learned that thumping in his chest was called his heart. Anytime it raced or skipped a beat, he investigated the cause to determine if it was the spark. When he'd sat next to Willow Conway in his parents' basement, his heart had raced, but they had been watching a horror movie at the time. He hadn't been scared of the monster rushing at the victims with his bloody blade. No, Porco had caught sight of

Annalee Walton sitting - on the floor, and his pulse had quickened to her.

In the skate park, he'd caught Shawna Welsh watching him do a kickflip, and his heart had raced. When he landed, Terri Clarke had winked at him, and he'd drooled after her for a couple of days.

He'd chased that spark of feeling from girl to girl. Sometimes it was strong, and he'd feel heat down in the base of his spine. Other times it was a weak tingling in his fingertip. It was never all-consuming, and the feeling never lasted like it had with his parents.

With Rosalind, his mouth had gone dry, and he'd drooled over the woman at the same time. She was a looker, easily the prettiest girl in the whole town. Although Paige Wiley, who had just moved to town, was giving Rosalind a run for the money in the looks department. Porco had chatted Paige up the other day while he was in town. He'd gotten her number and had asked her out for the weekend. He'd planned to break up with Rosalind before the date, of course. But then Rosalind had gone and dumped him first.

"Why are we even having this conversation?" asked Spinelli. "Just move onto the next one like you always do."

"Like I always do?"

"You've dated three different women since we've been here."

Here was the Vance Ranch in a small town in Montana. Though Porco wasn't sure how the town could be called small when a small ranch spanned farther than the eye could see. Porco and five of his Army Ranger buddies had opened a bootcamp training facility that bordered the Vance Ranch and the Purple Heart Ranch, a rehabilitation ranch for wounded veterans and their families.

The original plan had been to set up living quarters on the Purple Heart Ranch. That was, until the soldiers had learned of a little loophole that bade any man or woman who wanted to live on the Purple Heart Ranch for more than three months be bound in holy matrimony.

The regulation hadn't scared Porco. He wanted to get married. But only to the right girl. Whom he'd only find once he waded through all the firecracker dates and found his final, life-starting Big Bang.

"Your problem is you're always looking at the grass on the other side," Spinelli was saying. "You need to tend your own yard first."

"Well, that's what we're out here doing, isn't it."

Spinelli closed the drone's controller box and

handed the device to Porco. There were two drones on the ground, each housed a canister at its underbelly. The canisters were filled with chemical fertilizer for the barren pasture before them.

The two Army Rangers were helping out the owners of Vance Ranch. One of those owners being their former unit commander. Though they weren't on the lands of the Purple Heart Ranch, Sergeant Anthony Keaton had married Brenda Vance the same day he'd met the female rancher. It had been a marriage of convenience at first, one that allowed practical-minded Brenda to cut through the red tape of transferring land ownership of a parcel of Vance Ranch to tactical minded Keaton. Those two individuals had burned through their practical-tactical motivations a few moments after they said *I do* and were fast-tracked on the path to love.

Porco had asked Keaton what it felt like the moment he saw Brenda. Keaton had said he'd seen stars. Spinelli had pointed out the fact that Keaton had just been in a car accident with a ramming bull when he'd looked up to see Brenda racing towards him on a horse. As far as Porco was concerned, that still proved that there was a spark when The One stepped onto life's stage.

"Why'd she do it?" asked Spinelli. "Why'd she break up with you?"

Porco just stopped himself from asking Who? Had he forgotten about Rosalind so quickly? "She said I have a short attention span. She said she wanted to get out before I dropped her."

Spinelli pushed his lower lip up to meet his upper lip as though he could fathom that reason. "She has a point."

Spinelli had a scientific mind. He'd likely think a woman's spine was a looker or her brain had the tempting curves of a backroad. It wasn't that smarts weren't Porco's speed. Nothing made his heart skip like the sparkle of a woman's eyes. Nothing made his hand's itch more than running his fingers through lush curls. Nothing made his mouth water more than the tug of a plump, heart-shaped lip just begging to be kissed.

He'd felt all those things with Rosalind. If given time, could those flares feed into a bigger fire? "There was something there. We did have a spark of... something."

"You and that spark. You do realize that if you light a match, eventually it burns out."

That was Spinelli. The man always had to get scientific and ruin the emotions of the situation.

"Forget about Rosalind," Spinelli called as he mounted his horse, the controller to his drone in one hand, the reins in the other. "We have work to do. Remember, don't get too close to the border. That's the Verona Commune. We don't want any issues with them. Their crops are organic vegetables and..."

Spinelli droned on with his scientific talk as Porco mounted his own horse. They'd promised Brenda that they'd get the west pasture fertilized. The cattle ranch operation was growing, and this field had been running fallow too long. If the expansion was going to continue, they needed this field to produce so the cows could graze.

With a flick of his thumb, the drone lifted up into the sky. Porco kept himself and his mare a good distance behind the craft. The fertilizer wasn't toxic to humans, but he wasn't interested in having the chemicals for breakfast. He'd already had two plates of bacon. If he was lucky, there'd still be some on the stove when he got back.

It might have been a coincidence that he'd been born with that last name. Or it may have been a divine plan. Whatever it was, it was a happy accident that David Porco had grown to love all things pork.

Thinking of the greasy, crispy, sweet delightfulness that was bacon, Porco noticed too late that the drone had veered slightly off course. The craft hovered just over the border, where a wooden fence divided the two ranches. But the fence wasn't necessary to identify the boundary. The grass on the other side was definitely lusher, greener.

The drone flew for another few yards over the lush pasture, raining down the chemical compound. Porco gave the controller a couple of whacks until finally, the drone obeyed his commands and flew straight.

From his vantage point atop the horse, Porco couldn't see any damage that the drone had left on the fields. Just a small spray of fertilizer. With the overgrown weeds in the field, he doubted any of the hippies on the commune would even notice.

No harm, no foul.

He turned his horse away from the green pastures of the neighbors and continued on his journey. His mind was set on how to win back the woman who just might, maybe, possibly be the one. But first, he'd have to call and cancel his date with Paige.

## CHAPTER TWO

"Ay, me." Jules Capulano sighed as she looked down at the thriving plants in her garden.

Her woeful sigh wasn't over the abundance of green life surrounding her. Her beloved soybeans had grown nearly tall enough to reach her knees. The leaves stretched out as though to wave at her. The bulbous pods hung heavy as though the beans inside were ready to drop and harvest themselves.

Life was good for the crops on the Verona Commune. Her belly was full every meal from the fresh fruits and vegetables her fellow vegans harvested each day. Her ears were filled with the laughter of the third generation of children running wild and barefoot across acres and acres of land. It was only her heart that was empty.

"Ay, me." She sighed again.

"Oh, no," came a withering sigh that mirrored the tone and tenor of Jules's own voice. "Are you about to enter into a longwinded monologue filled with Elizabethan slang?"

Jules pushed her long, interwoven locks back off her forehead to look up at Romey. Unlike Jules's coiled twists that reached down her back toward the earth, her sister's hair was short and springy, her curls reaching for the sunlight. Romey's butterscotch skin had tanned to caramel under the sun's constant attention.

Since their shared birthday, the Capulano twins woke up with the sun and spent all day in its rays, coming in only once the moon rained its dark light on their parade. While out in the fields, Jules would sprinkle flower seeds as she danced barefoot in the dirt. Where Romey would trough equidistant lines and space out her seedlings in neat little rows.

Their planting methods weren't the only thing different about the twins. Although born identical, it had always been easy to tell the two apart. Jules dressed in colorful sundresses every day of her life, where Romey tugged on funny t-shirts and shorts.

Today's graphic tee displayed two atoms. The bubble over the first element said *I lost an electron*. The second element asked, *Are you positive*?

"If you're going to recite Shakespeare, at least cite *Cymbeline*," said Romey. "There's science in that play."

Jules had heard enough of that little-known Shakespearian play recited by Romey and their historian father, who specialized in the Elizabethan era, when she was younger. The play mentioned a few references to cosmology, which the two would debate endlessly on whether the playwright had read Galileo. Jules retreated to the corner of their cottage home, preferring to read the bard's sonnets instead.

"There's romance, too," Jules insisted. Though she quickly regretted taking the bait.

"Sure there is; adultery, incest, attempted rape, attempted murder, more lies, and deception. I keep telling you, romance belongs on the page and not in real life. That stuff could get you killed. You should be practical about these things."

Practical? Nothing in their lives was practical. Everything had been to the extremes.

Take their parents, for example. In what world would an African American man from the south who was obsessed with all things from Queen Elizabeth's reign fall in love with a radical, white feminist, from a small town in Maine, who'd tried—in vain—to join the Black Panther Party. If their parents had been practical and hadn't believed in the power of true love, neither Jules nor Romey would be here today.

"Paris said he'd give us a ride to the county fair," said Romey.

"Ay, me," Jules groaned. She should've known this was where the conversation would head.

Paris Montgomery wasn't a bad guy. Far from it. He was kind and jovial. Any girl would love to have his attention. Jules was one of them.

She'd loved playing with Paris when they were kids. The three of them, Paris, Romey, and Jules had grown up close; practically brother and sisters since their parents had founded this commune over twenty years ago. From a young age, Jules remembered the adults joking about one of the twins and Paris falling in love and marrying.

Early on, they'd ruled out Romey. Jules's twin was far more interested in books than boys. And not the romantic books. Romey preferred the nonfiction section of the commune's library. That left Jules. But

Jules had only ever seen Paris as a brother. Not a lover.

Love was fireworks in the heart. Love was the eyes shining bright when looking upon the one meant for you. Love was an itch in the palm of the hands to reach out and hold on forever.

Jules's hands met with a hairy back and wrinkled flesh. When she turned to face the newcomer, she had to immediately turn away and wrinkle her nose at the smell.

"Hamlet, how did you get out?"

In response to her question, Jules got an enthusiastic *oink*, along with a wiggle of his fat rump. Hamlet, their pet pig, thought he was a dog. His three-hundred-pound weight slowed him down as he tried to race after them all over the commune, but it never lessened his enthusiasm to catch up to them. What surprised Jules the most was that the pig never seemed to lose an ounce of weight despite how much he trailed after humans and the fact that he was on the same vegan diet as the rest of the families who lived on the lands.

Jules gave the pig a scratch behind the ears and was rewarded with hearty squeals of delight. The pig's murmuring of appreciation was accompanied by a buzzing sound. Bees weren't too common in this part of the commune as soybeans were self-pollinating plants. Listening harder, Jules noted that the sound was coming from above.

Looking up, she quickly found the source of the buzzing. Off in the distance, beyond their property line, a small aircraft flew.

“Is that a toy airplane?” said Jules.

Romey used her hand to shield her gaze before announcing, “Looks like a drone. I guess the soldiers are out playing at war this morning.”

There were three ranches in this part of the valley beyond the town. The Purple Heart Ranch was filled to the brim with soldiers, most of them wounded veterans who’d come to the ranch to heal from their time in combat. Jerome Capulano had been a pacifist, but his wife Mariam had been a full-on antiwar advocate. Even though Mariam, along with most of the commune, had waged a decade's long war with the ranch that sat between the Verona Commune and the Purple Heart Ranch.

The Vance Ranch.

The Vances were cattle farmers. The fact that their trade was in meat was bad enough. What was worse was that for years the Vances had been using fertilizer to grow their pastures for their cows to feed on. They had no care for their neighbors who abhorred the use of unnatural chemicals in their foods or near their homes.

Words had been exchanged. There was a rumor that a couple of blows had been thrown between Paris's dad and old Mr. Vance. Jules could easily imagine it. Heathcliff Montgomery had a fiery temper, a booming voice, and meaty fists. Eventually, lawsuits had been filed. Now existed a fragile peace between the current Vance head rancher, who was a woman, and Paris, who'd taken over the leadership position of the commune.

Paris was nothing like his father. The young man had a quiet voice that people hushed to listen to, a ready encouragement for any child he came near, and a thumb greener than the plants that he tended.

He really was a catch. Jules only hoped that someday the right woman would snatch him up. She was not the one to cast that net.

The drone continued zigging off course, heading back deeper into Vance Ranch territory and out of Jules's sight.

"You're trying to change the subject," Romey was saying. "Papa and Paris's dad thought you two would marry. You two have gotten closer these past few months working on the organic certification."

Romey was right about that. Jules and Paris had

gotten closer as they'd begun preparations to have the commune's lands certified as organic by the USDA. But working that closely with him day in and out made things crystal clear to Jules.

"I don't love him, Romey. I mean, I love him, like a brother. But I've never gotten goosebumps when I see him. He's never made my heart speed up. Or put butterflies in my stomach."

"All of that is scientific nonsense."

"You have no sense of imagination."

"That's not imagination you're describing. It's a medical condition."

Jules stood, aiming to get away from her sister and her logic. But she knew better. Once Romey did the math and came to a solution, she dug her heels in until everyone became convinced that hers was the right answer. Luckily, Hamlet was a hefty buffer between the sisters.

"Marrying Paris is a good business decision," said Romey. "It was our parents that founded this commune."

"Marriage shouldn't be a business transaction."

"That's exactly what it is. That's exactly how it developed. Disney movies changed all that with its princesses. That's why I prefer Pixar."

Jules didn't bother responding. Just because they

were twins and shared the same looks that didn't mean they shared the same brain. Jules was determined to find true love, just like in the storybooks. Just like her namesake. Only without the poison and suicide bit.

# CHAPTER THREE

The smells of the county fair were all around him. Growing up in the city, Porco had been to carnivals and amusement parks. He'd been jostled about through the frenzy of busy people rushing their children through the long waiting lines of rides. Or paying fees near the cost of entry to skip to the front of the lines. Only to come off the ride and hurry to make it to the next appointment of hectic diversion.

A small town fair was a unique experience. There was rushing about. But only by the young who were hopped up on sugared candies and fizzy drinks. The adults strolled leisurely, conversing with one another, waving to friends, literally stopping to smell the roses as they checked out a florist's booth.

"There really is no such thing as love."

Porco pressed his lips together rather than to address Spinelli's comment. Spinelli was the smartest guy he knew. The man could compute large equations in seconds without the use of a calculator, or even pen or paper. He could remember minute details and call them forth in the heat of a battle. He was handy with tools and anything mechanical bowed to his whim.

But the man was hopeless when it came to anything to do with the fairer sex. In fact, Porco couldn't remember a single time Spinelli had been out on a date.

"What you're feeling is simply a cocktail of adrenaline, dopamine, and serotonin increasing in levels," Spinelli went on. "It's the same chemicals released on the battlefield."

"So, what you're saying is love is a battlefield?"

"No," Spinelli answered, not even acknowledging the righteous use of the lyrics from Pat Benatar's girl-power anthem. "I'm saying your fight or flight reaction is triggered. There are two choices in that scenario. Ever think you keep making the wrong one?"

Yeah, that had to be why the guy hadn't had a single date the whole time Porco had known him.

When he'd met Spinelli, the guy was barely a hundred pounds wet. The heaviest thing on him had been his brain. All these years later, and the Rangers had added what Spinelli had in his IQ to his muscle mass.

Stepping up to a booth that sold battered and fried bacon on a stick, Porco bought two. Spinelli waved the heaven-sent concoction off, as Porco knew the health-conscious man would. Which meant more for him.

His waistline would not appreciate him even if his belly did. Now that he was out of the service, he didn't have to worry about things like weight. Though he doubted it would matter now that the camp was open and they were running drills every weekday and Saturday.

"So, what?" Porco said, picking up the thread of their conversation. "You'll never want to settle down with a woman, buy a house, have a family of your own?"

"I do. But I'd go about both processes in the same way," said Spinelli. "When you look for a home, it has to meet certain specifications; a certain square footage, the right amenities, cost."

"You'd pick the woman you'll marry based on a property report and home inspection?"

Spinelli shrugged. "Isn't that essentially what online dating is? Far more logical than relying on a spike in blood flow."

"I can't wait until love smacks you dead in the face."

"You'll be waiting forever since the concept doesn't have hands. And you're missing the point; you don't love Rosalind."

Didn't he? Porco was no longer sure. He knew he'd felt something with her. Otherwise, he'd be able to get her out of his mind easily. Since he couldn't, he owed it to himself to be sure. He just needed to find her first.

Porco finished off the second skewer of bacon, licking his chops. All along the main street of the fair were more booths touting deep-fried concoctions. Maple bacon donuts. Waffle fried bacon. Bacon stuffed burgers. He'd definitely have to come back and try the chocolate-covered bacon.

But first, he had important business to attend to. He set his feet toward the other end of the park, where he knew Rosalind would be.

He didn't miss the giggles and stares of some women. He sidestepped a few who frowned. Those frowners were girls he'd danced with for a night or dated for a weekend when he first got here. He hadn't felt a spark with Bonnie Jones or Crystal Bates. He didn't believe in keeping a woman hanging when there was no fire between them. He was decent like that.

Up ahead, Porco caught sight of the woman whom he still held a torch for. At least he thought it was a torch. He definitely felt something warm lick up his spine. But he couldn’t gauge the temperature from this distance. He needed to get closer.

From this distance, he could see that Rosalind was dressed in her customary plaid shirt with a bit of lace on the collar. Cowgirl chic. She wore a Stetson as usual, so Porco could see her shining blue eyes. Or wait? Were they gray? He couldn’t remember.

He could see her long blonde hair. Though the strands hung a bit limp in the midday sun. She was smiling, but the expression didn't quite reach her eyes. Come to think of it, he couldn't remember her smile ever being wider than what he saw now.

"David."

Uh oh. Things weren't good when any of his fellow soldiers called him by his first name. It was much like when his mother said his first and middle name through gritted teeth.

Porco turned to glare at Spinelli. The man

looked as though he'd been talking for a while. But Porco's attention had been otherwise occupied.

"I'm just trying to help,“ said Spinelli.

"By keeping me from the woman who might be The One."

Spinelli let his head roll around his neck, the tendons popping along the journey. "You realize the two of you have nothing in common."

"You realize opposites attract. Isn't that a scientific fact?"

"For magnets. But if one flips around, they repel one another."

"I don't see your point?"

"Yeah, I know." Spinelli rolled his neck the other way. Fewer tendons popped this time. At the end of the journey, his head hung low. He raised his hand in a magnanimous gesture and flicked his fingers. "Go on. You'll lose interest by the weekend. There's a bet on it. I have my money on tomorrow morning."

"Some friend you are." Porco turned on his heel and stormed away.

"That would be your best one you've got," Spinelli called after him.

Porco made up the ground between him and his target quickly. Spinelli was wrong. He and Rosalind were like magnets. He could feel a gravitational pull towards this woman.

Though he was drawn to her, the object of his desire wasn't looking at him. Rosalind was smiling still. Her smile stretched a bit higher this time. Porco wanted to know why? Who had made her smile this big? His glance slid over to Rosalind's companion, and his heart stopped.

It had been a sunny day, but the star shifted. The rays moved across the sky to shine down on the single bright spot before him. Everyone around *her* was cast in shadows in Porco's eyes.

The noisy fairgrounds quieted to a hum in his ears. Overhead, he heard birds chirping the sweetest melody as though they were playing a chorus to make way for *her* appearance on life's stage.

Standing across from the woman Porco thought he'd fallen for was the woman he knew had captured his heart.

She wore a sundress in a riot of rainbow colors. Her skin was a light golden brown, like the battered fried bacon skewers he'd just wolfed down. He'd bet she'd taste as sweet as the honeyed ham. He was determined to find out because one word kept playing in his head over and over again.

*Mine.*

## CHAPTER FOUR

"That natural pomade has done wonders for my hair." Rosalind Carr ran her polished nails through her long, silky hair.

Jules smiled and nodded at Rosalind's words. Her blonde tresses did look much healthier than the first time Jules had met her a few months back at the weekly farmer's market. Back then, the rodeo queen's ends had been split and ragged from all the time spent under hairdryers and the exposure to harsh chemicals and dyes to keep her looking like a natural blonde.

"It's never been this healthy and fine," Rosalind beamed down at her hair, as though she were talking to the strands. "I swear it's grown at least three inches in the last two months."

"That would be the aloe vera plant giving you the moisture," said Jules. "The nettles and rosemary promote growth."

They grew each of the herbs in the southern part of the commune. The soil there was more gritty, which suited the Mediterranean plants best. Harmony Sunshine, Verona's resident herbalist, took pride in getting the most exotic specimens to thrive in the midwest.

"That River Sunshine is a genius," said Rosalind. "Is he here today? I'd love to get my hands on some more."

"River is no longer a he, remember? She transitioned earlier this year and changed her name to Harmony."

It had been a beautiful rebirthing ceremony out at the stream that ran through the northern part of their property. Harmony's mother, a poet laureate, performed a heartfelt spoken-word piece about letting the waters in her son's heart reverse course, and now her daughter lived in harmony. Jules choked up just thinking about it.

"Oh, I don't care if he's gay," Rosalind insisted. She pressed her hand to her heart and spread her fingers wide over her chest as though she was showing that the organ was open. "It's very progressive of him. I mean her? Of them?"

Jules knew that the way she'd grown up was a strong pill for many in this community to follow. In a land of cattle and hog ranches, those who lived on Verona abhorred the thought of slaughter for food or clothes. In a town where the churches were packed every Sunday, the open fields on the commune held shrines to every god, goddess, and pagan saint known to mankind -because they didn't want to leave any deity out.

Many of the townsfolk frowned at their ways. No one had ever raised a fist or a foul word. Well, except the Vances and the Montgomerys. Outside of that ongoing feud, the people of the town had tried often to welcome the residents of the commune, albeit in their awkward, see-look-I'm-openminded-just-don't-go-too-far, kinda way.

"Harmony isn't here today, but we do have some of her products out at our booth."

Rosalind's eyes lit up. She looked up, turning her head in the direction of the Verona booth where they'd laid out a store of fresh produce. If she walked over there, Rosalind would find the homemade hair products she coveted, along with hand-fashioned jewelry, scarves, hats, and other articles of clothing crocheted or knitted from natural fibers, and organic fruits and vegetables.

Jules just hoped Rosalind didn't ask her to accompany her back there. She'd driven with Paris to the fair. For the first time in their lives, there had been an awkward silence between the two of them. They'd both tried to fill that silence with familiar topics like the progress of her soybeans, the upcoming commune community meeting which was always lively with debate, the impending visit from the USDA inspector over the organic seal of approval for their produce.

They'd exchanged only a few sentences. The weight of the words unsaid was heavy in the cab of his fuel-efficient hybrid truck. The tension prickled across her skin, causing her to shiver in discomfort. The tense silence had given Jules a moment to study her longtime friend, who wanted to be her lifelong mate.

Paris Montgomery was handsome. He had a strong chin and high cheekbones that could belong to a model. Though he was never one to go in front of a camera. His body was lean from his plant-based diet, and muscular from his work in the fields each day.

He was a quiet man, had been so ever since they

were children. A gentler soul than his fiery father who had been a professional protestor in his youth, Paris preferred plants to people. Jules was much the same. It wouldn't be all bad if she chose to marry him.

Something squeezed in her heart, like the valves of the organ were wringing its hands with worry and anxiety. Perhaps that was why she'd shot out of the passenger seat as soon as he'd parked. Maybe that was why she'd walked away from the booth and made herself scarce for the last hour.

"Oh, no. Not him."

The words hadn't come from Jules's distressed heart. They'd come from Rosalind. The light of excitement over hair care had faded from Rosalind's gaze. Her perfectly plucked brow was now pinched in annoyance.

Had Paris come up to them? Had he come in search of Jules, ready to break his silence? Was he now standing behind Jules? What if he was down on one knee?

There were prickles all over her skin. But these weren't the prickles from before. They weren't uncomfortable pinches. They felt like sparklers dancing up her forearms, sliding across her shoulder blades, and racing down her back.

Jules's heart gave a mighty kick to the front of her chest, as though calling all her organs to attention. Every part of her was on high alert. Her ears rang clear. Her ten fingers felt a tingle. The soles of her feet were grounded where she stood.

Another mighty kick of her heart. This time she knew that something urged her to turn around. It wasn't a fight or flight sense of urgency. Jules couldn't quite put her finger on what the sensation was. She just knew that she had to turn if she wanted to live.

And so, she did.

First, her head. Her gaze pushed her peripheral vision to its max, trying to get a closer look at what was to come. It was only a glimpse, but she saw the next chapter of her life unfolding as her head, then her shoulders, then her entire body came around.

The man standing over her blocked out the sun, but Jules had never felt so hot in her life. His gaze bored into her, as though it saw directly into her soul. She felt bare and confused at the same time as she felt completely cloaked and understood.

There were no sparks when the man smiled. No, there was an explosion in that devilish grin. A raging fire ignited as everything in Jules shouted two words; *this one.*

## CHAPTER FIVE

The first thing Porco had learned to do in Basic Training was to march. Forward March was the command given when standing at a halt. They had been taught to pick up their left foot, taking one step measuring from the heel to the toe. The right arm should coordinate in a swing. Arms straight but not stiff. Hands cupped, thumbs pointing down. A coordinated effort with each soldier moving in unison.

Porco lifted his right foot. His right arm swung at the same time, making his body appear as though it lurched forward, casting him off balance. Each of his fingers stretched out, wanting, needing to grab hold of *her*.

With a few more strides forward, his limbs fell

into synchronized motion. Left, right, then left. Porco marched towards his glory.

He was drawn by her hazel eyes. Even from this distance, he saw that there were gold flecks at the edges of her pupils. Their sparkle rivaled that of the sun. Her lips were the perfect shape of a heart, lush and round. He doubted that there was any gloss from a tube coating the flesh there. It had to be her natural coloring. Between her lips and her eyes, her cheeks were flecked with freckles. Not the pale pink he'd seen on other women's skin. The collection of dots was mocha swirls on her caramel skin. Porco had the urge to lean down and sip at the sprinkles.

To get to her cheeks, he'd have to brush away the thick strands of her hair that partially hid her face from view. Much of her hair was coiled up atop her head, but in the back, the dark ropes rioted and fell down her back, reaching the base of her spine. The locks of hair were threaded through like the crochet work he'd seen his grandma make.

Dreadlocks, the style was called. There was nothing dreadful about the way they looked. Porco ached to reach his hand out and test their texture. He wanted to know if they were as silky as they appeared to be.

"Yes, David? Is there something I can help you with?"

Porco's mouth had been agape as he'd taken in the sight of this angel on earth. His lips flattened at the wince at the sound of that voice. He'd expected his angel's voice to shimmer like stardust. Not grind like the gears of a vehicle when downshifted.

Aside from the tenor of her voice was its tone. There was annoyance there, tinged with exasperation.

She was mad at him? But she hadn't even met him yet. And how did she know his name?

Gazing down at her, Porco realized her lips hadn't moved. It was not her voice that had spoken. It was Rosalind. Porco had completely forgotten the other woman was there.

Rosalind shifted, placing her body between Porco's and the woman who had captured his entire attention. With her move, Rosalind also blocked out the sun, casting a shadow on the portion of his dream girl that Porco could still see.

The object of his desire was still gazing back at him beneath hooded lids. Was she shy? Even if she was, Porco saw interest in those sparkling eyes. He opened his mouth to speak to her, but the English language eluded him.

What did one say to an angel?

"I hope you haven't come here to cause a scene," Rosalind was saying.

Porco's angel's brows drew in a frown. Her bright gaze dimmed, and she pulled her lower lip into her mouth. He had to swallow a couple of times, just to reign in some sense. He needed to get rid of Rosalind. He couldn't even remember why he'd come over to her in the first place.

"I'm surprised you've even come over here to talk to me," said Rosalind. "I figured you'd already be onto the next girl."

His angel's gaze widened at that. Not wanting any more dirt kicked up to mar his character, Porco found his voice. Unfortunately, the first word his angel would hear him utter was a curse. The foul word made her wince, and Porco cursed again, only under his breath this time.

"I'm not here for you, Rosalind," he said, finally turning to address his ex.

One of Rosalind's perfectly plucked brows lifted. Was there disappointment there in her ice-blue eyes? Porco didn't care. He couldn't remember what he'd seen in her in the first place.

On the few dates they'd been on, she'd never missed looking into any window or reflective glass they'd walked by. Whenever he'd reached for her hand, he'd have to first disentangle her fingers from her hair. He couldn't remember a single thing they'd talked about when they were together.

"I'm surprised you even remember my name," Rosalind said. "I heard you'd already moved onto the new girl in town."

Porco glanced at the angel standing behind his ex. Her gaze was averted, as though she were trying not to listen. Of course, she'd heard every word. Not one of them had been flattering towards Porco. He hadn't canceled the date with Paige. And right now, he definitely had different plans.

"That is your reputation after all," Rosalind continued her attack. "Love them and leave them. I just left you first is all."

"I wasn't going to..." Porco didn't finish that sentence. Because that was exactly what he'd already done. But it was only because he'd felt a true spark with...

Wait! Where did she go? Porco turned right and then left and then all the way around. To no avail. His angel was gone.

"You want to date *her*," sniffed Rosalind. "Fat chance. You'll never get anywhere near her."

"Who is she? What's her name?"

"Trust me, I'm doing you a favor." Rosalind chuckled low. She crossed her arms over her chest. Her plucked brows narrowed in triumph. The dark outline of her eye makeup cast her in a sinister light. "That one is completely out of your league."

Out of his league? What did she mean by that? It wasn't like Porco had never struck out before. It just didn't happen often. He had a natural way with women. At the end of the day, he only wanted to have his way with one; the right one.

Could his angel be that girl?

"No, actually, she's not even on the same planet as you."

"Look, Rosalind, I'm sorry things didn't work out between us."

"Save it." Rosalind held up her hand. "I'm going to sit back and enjoy you chase after her and fall flat on your face for once. She'll never date a guy like you."

A guy like him? What did she mean by that? But Rosalind was already walking away, cackling as she went.

Porco didn't bother following after her. He turned and headed left. It had to be the direction his dream girl had gone.

A few moments later he was proven right when he spotted her. Out of his league? To the contrary.

She was standing at the deep-fried pork station looking up at the menu with wide eyes. It was as though the stars were aligning. She was perfect for him.

# CHAPTER SIX

Jules grimaced, trying not to inhale too deeply. The smell of meat and sugar frying in day-old oil was doing tricks in her stomach. That, and her head was spinning from the encounter she'd walked away from. For much of the conversation between Rosalind and that man, David was his name.

David.

She liked that name. It was a strong, competent name. To even utter it she had to bite her lip when her mouth formed the V at the center of it.

David.

She didn't say his name out loud now. It whispered in her mind. Still, in reality, she bit her lip. A tingle crept across each of her pinky fingers, moving from her left hand all the way to her right. A shudder skittered down her spine as she stood in the noonday sun.

Her heart thumped. Her mind whirled. It had happened.

She'd always thought that when she felt it -that spark- that it would be like floating on a cloud.

It wasn't.

When she'd come face to face with David, it had been like an explosion. With each step he took nearer to her, smaller bursts of aftershocks had set off all along her body. It was as though her goosebumps had been boobytrapped.

Her breath had left her in a whoosh. Her belly had turned a somersault -not like a child turning a cartwheel. More like a gymnast stomping into the mat after a series of flips where they land with their hands over their heads. Her own knees would not have allowed her to stick such a landing. They'd gone to Jell-O.

He'd looked down upon her with those dark eyes that felt like a flashlight shining directly into her. Jules had wanted to shield her gaze, but she couldn't look away from him.

Once she and David had breathed the same air, everything around her had stopped. She felt weary and energized, and worn and whole, tired and wide awake all at the same time.

So that was him. That was the guy who had made her heart kick into high gear. That was the man her soul recognized as it's missing part. And, to hear Rosalind tell it, it turned out he was some kind of player.

Great. Of all the luck.

Aside from her hair care needs, Jules didn't know Rosalind well. She knew that the woman was strong-minded and independent. As a woman who tussled with raging bulls, wild horses, and randy cowboys for a living, Jules figured Rosalind didn't suffer fools easily. She was the type of woman that men chased after. So if she dismissed David as a lady's man, it was very likely that he was indeed community property.

Jules had lived her life in a community where everything was shared. Her clothes were hand-me-downs. All meals were potluck fare. For once in her life, she'd wanted something of her own.

She'd thought that when she fell in love, it would be once and forever. Not for a moment with a man who had been passed around by the entire town. Her heart had to be wrong about him. Her soul had made a mistake.

Jules let go of her bottom lip. She would not be saying his name again. Not in her mind or in life.

"Hi."

Her two front teeth reached out and snagged the plump flesh at the corner of her mouth. Her heart *tap-tapped* in her chest, ignoring her mind's determination. Heat blasted from her very soul, letting her know that her life would never be the same the moment she turned to that voice.

And she was going to turn around. It was inevitable. Because fate was not going to be ignored.

David towered over her. He was easily six and a half feet tall. She hadn't noticed his height at first. Jules was a tall girl, and most of the boys on the commune barely came up to her chin.

Not David. He had a good foot over her. He made her feel... Well, not small.

Instinctively, she knew that he was the kind of man that would keep her safe and protected. She had the urge to step into his arms and nuzzle her nose right into his chest because that's where her head would fit.

He held out his hand. Had he read her mind? Was he giving her an invitation to do just that?

"I'm David."

Jules gulped once, then twice. Swallowing down

her out of control desires. She took the proffered hand. The moment their fingertips touched, she felt another set of explosions go off. This time the blast tripped up her arm and set off fireworks in her heart.

Looking up into his eyes, she could've sworn she saw sparkles reflected back at her. His lips parted as he looked down at her. His hand was warm as it enclosed hers. The aftershocks of the bomb were gone now. All that remained was a warm glow between them.

“My name is Julia."

David smiled like he liked her name. He repeated it quietly, as though testing it out on his tongue. Jules loved the sound of her name coming from his mouth. But something wasn’t quite right about the way he said it.

"Everyone calls me Jules."

Yes. That was it. She liked the way he said Jules even better.

"I'm David."

She grinned shyly. “You said."

He nodded, tugging at the corner of his upper lip with his teeth as though searching for something more to say. “Everyone calls me Porco."

Jules wrinkled her nose at that. She knew kids were cruel. Had he been overweight growing up? If the nickname was a taunt, she certainly wasn't going to participate in the teasing.

"I like David."

"Then David, it is."

"David?"

"Yes, Jules?"

"Are you going to give me back my hand?"

They were standing in front of the long lines of the fried food station. People moved around them to get into and out of the line with their crispy, brown foodstuffs. Jules noted that she was no longer having trouble breathing in the oily smells.

"No," David said.

"No, you're not going to give me back my hand?"

He shook his head in the negative, but his lips curled in a smile. A possessive smile. The warmth emanating from that smile made another trek up to her arm and pulsed in her chest. David's nostrils flared as though he'd sensed what he did to her.

"You feel it too, don't you?" he said.

Jules didn't pretend to not know what he was talking about. In answer, she gave a little nod of her head. It was all the movement she could muster being held in his gaze, being held in the palm of his hand.

“I do,” she whispered.

David's palm pressed firmly against hers. His thumb rubbed at the skin of her knuckles. Never in her life had Jules felt so cared for with such a simple gesture.

The moment was so big and life-altering. But, also light and natural. It was exactly how she dreamed meeting him would be. Except for the sizzling pig meat surrounding them.

She wanted to get away from here. To be alone with him. To know everything about him. Looking up, she saw an impediment to that desire.

In the distance, she saw her twin. Romey hadn't spotted Jules. Because Romey's face was turned. She was chatting with Paris.

"I have to go," Jules said.

Jules snatched her hand from David. She only got her palm free. But David held onto her fingers.

"You can't go. I just found you."

Her gymnast's heart flipped from one side of her chest to the other, sticking another boisterous landing.

David stepped closer to her. His gaze intent on her face. Then his eyes narrowed on her lips.

The world stopped. Everything centered on him, where his five fingers held onto her, where his dark eyes focused on her. She knew without any shadow of a doubt that her life would be entwined with this man. She just had to take care of one thing first.

"I'll come back," she said. "I just need to handle a family matter first."

"I'll let you go," he said. "But I'm going to wait here for you."

"Right here?" she grinned, looking at their surroundings. The overly sweet scent of deep-fried batter and pork made her senses rear back. David didn't seem to notice.

"Right here." He planted both feet and smiled down at her. "Promise you'll come back?"

"I promise."

That was all it took. David let her go. She could make her escape. Leaving him was the last thing she wanted to do, but she had to go and talk to the two most important people in her life to let them know that her life had irrevocably changed forever.

## CHAPTER SEVEN

He was on top of the world. Her last words to him, her promise, felt like a vow. Like a solemn oath that had left him anything but sober. Porco felt drunk as he walked through the fair.

His footfalls were aimless. His only goal, his only care was to will the hands of the clock to move faster. He itched to reach up and push the sundown, tucking it under the cover of darkness so that night might rise, and Jules would return to him.

Jules, his heart sighed.

What an appropriate name for her. She had been a jewel in his eyes. He'd known she was precious after his first glance at her. When he'd come to stand before her, her entire being had twinkled at him, and he’d become lost in her shimmer. Sparking his every nerve ending to life.

Jules, his mind exhaled.

For as long as he'd been dating, he'd never told another girl about the spark he'd felt when he'd met them. Thinking back on it, Porco started to wonder if what he'd felt all those other times had actually been anything other than idle curiosity. Nothing had ignited him before, like what he'd felt standing in her light.

Jules, whispered the hairs along his forearms.

With those eyes flecked with gold at the rim. With that skin of amber and lips of rubies. Her white teeth had flashed pearls as she smiled shyly at him. But he got the sense that she wasn’t shy. Only as startled as he was to feel the undeniable pull between them.

He'd seen the moment she'd felt something between them. Her eyes had gone wide with surprise as his had done. She couldn't deny it. Not even after Rosalind's words when she'd turned away from him. That would be the last time his jewel would walk away from him. Porco vowed it.

If she’d doubted him then he would never give her heart another reason to falter, her feet another cause to back away. Porco would show Jules that no other woman would ever touch her shine.

"Hey, Porco. Wanna come on a ride with us?"

Porco looked up to find two women rising up into the sky. A honey blonde girl in a too-tight tank top. And an ebony-skinned brunette with a cowboy hat pulled over her long, wavy tresses. They sat in one booth of the Ferris wheel. The ride lifted them up off the ground, rising toward the sun. Had it been another day, Porco might have leaped onto the ride, causing it to rock. Causing the women to giggle with delight at his daring.

He turned away from them and moved on. That ride, those girls, neither could lift him any higher off the ground than the mere thought of Jules's return. But the sun hadn't given a single inch of its position in the sky.

Jules, his entire being wanted to howl.

"How's Rosalind?"

Porco stumbled to a halt. Rusty leaned against the railing of a petting zoo. The words Vance Ranch were proudly displayed along the fencing. Inside the zoo, young calves roamed the perimeter. Their heads dipped low as their mouths fed at the bales of hay laid next to the wooden posts. Small, eager hands reached between the rails to pet heads and ears.

In the next enclosure were adult cows. Leaning against those rails, watching the cattle eat, were adult humans. Those buyers sized up the beasts, measuring their worth for an upcoming auction.

Rusty cleared his throat. Then snapped his fingers for good measure. The man looked over at Porco expectantly. Rusty had asked him a question. For the life of him, Porco couldn't remember the place or name Rusty had uttered.

"Who?" said Porco.

Rusty lifted his brows at the single word. He turned his puzzled gaze to Spinelli, who'd stepped up to join them. Spinelli's brows drew together as he regarded Porco, understanding in his intelligent gaze.

"He's already found someone new," Spinelli announced.

Rusty shook his head, pressing his lips together with what Porco knew was disappointment in him. Rusty hadn't dated much. He'd only been with one woman his entire life.

"Not a new girl," Porco corrected. "*The* girl. The last girl. The One."

Spinelli rolled his eyes. Porco was sure it was a perfect three-hundred-and-sixty-degree circle of disbelief. Rusty looked away. The man's belief in

The One had been damaged by the divorce papers his estranged wife had sent to him months ago. They sat awaiting his signature, tucked away in his duffel bag.

"I'm serious," insisted Porco. "I've never felt anything like this before. And she felt it too."

"What? The magical spark." Spinelli wiggled his fingers as though at the sky before letting them fall to his sides. "There's no such thing. It's just a heart palpitation. A biological response caused by stress, exertion, caffeine, alcohol, or hormones. The only way that would be magic would be if you're experiencing menstruation, pregnancy, or menopause."

Spinelli had to ruin everything was science and logic. Porco often wondered if the man was nothing more than a robot underneath those clothes. His brawn. as well as his brain too often resembled the cold of metal.

"No," Porco said with certainty. "What's between me and this woman is definitely magic."

"When did you meet her?" asked Rusty.

"Ten minutes ago."

Again, another look between his two friends.

"What do you know about her?" asked Rusty.

"She's beautiful," Porco grinned. But the grin

slipped as Spinelli opened his mouth, preparing to rain on Porco's parade. "She's responsible."

The only reason she'd left him was to handle a family matter. So, she held family in high regard. His mother always said to watch how his potential partner treated their parents to see how they would treat him. Although, Porco wasn't sure if Jules had gone off to help her parents or siblings or other relatives.

"Is that it?" asked Spinelli. "Is that all you know about this one."

"The One," Porco corrected. He knew that and that Jules had admitted that she felt it too. That was all he needed to know. "Love isn't science. It's emotion. I felt that spark with her. No, it was an explosion. And she felt it too. She told me so."

The wariness in Spinelli's eyes had Porco clenching his fist. The two of them had never come to blows before, but there was a first time for everything.

"What's her name?" asked Rusty, stepping between the two men.

"Jules."

"Jules?" said Rusty. "Do you mean Jules Capulano?"

Porco frowned. They hadn't exchanged last

names. But that didn't matter because one day her last name would be his.

“Jules Capulano?” said Spinelli, his gaze gone from wary to worry. “From the Verona Commune?"

She hadn't told him where she lived. Porco didn't like that his friends knew more about his dream girl than he did.

"Brown skin?” asked Rusty. “Long dreadlocks."

Porco nodded, though he didn't like that Rusty used the word dread to describe her hair. "Yeah, that's her."

Rusty winced and turned away. Spinelli whistled low and wrinkled his nose.

“What?” demanded Porco. What could they possibly have to say against the angel who had set his entire being aflame?

"You know she's vegan?" said Spinelli.

"So, you're racist now?" Porco accused. He wasn’t entirely sure what the word meant. He didn't care what race or religion she was.

“Vegan means she doesn’t eat meat,” said Rusty.

Was that all? Most women were picky when it came to what was on their plates. “So, we’ll eat seafood when we go out.”

Again, Rusty and Spinelli shared another look

that left Porco feeling on the outs about the woman he intended to woo.

"There's no way a relationship between you two would work," said Spinelli. "You're far too different."

So, both of his friends were prejudiced. Great. This was quickly turning into a scene from *Guess Who's Coming to Dinner*? Which made even less sense since both of his friends had mixed heritage in their blood. Spinelli's mother was from South America and his father from Italy. Where Rusty's mother had immigrated from Thailand when she was young.

"Doesn't matter to me what color her skin is or what god she worships or what she eats," said Porco. "She's the one for me, and that's all there is to it."

# CHAPTER EIGHT

"Where have you been?" demanded Romey. "Paris has been looking for you."

At present, Paris was chatting with a customer. He held up a crooked looking squash, patiently explaining that even though the vegetable wasn't the prettiest, the taste would be unlike anything the buyer had ever sampled. That was the reason their booth at the weekly farmer's markets had a never-ending line of repeat customers. No grocery store could top the taste of what they pulled from their organic fields.

With the sale made, Paris stuffed the money in the till. He lifted his head and their gazes connected. Jules could see the sharp intake of breath he took when he spotted her. Her breathing remained even. Paris swallowed and then displayed a wide grin as he regarded her. Jules tugged at one corner of her mouth, urging her lips to rise.

Even though Paris stood in the full light of the sun, she felt no heat between them. His attentions left her cool, unaffected. Jules needed to tell him that. She needed to let him know that she had no feelings for him, at least not in that way.

“Are you going to answer my question?” said Romey. “Where have you been?”

"Romey, you'll never guess what's just happened to me."

"What?" Romey scanned her sister’s body like a mother would after her child returned after a stint at the playground. "Are you hurt?"

Where the average twins were born moments apart, Romey was the elder twin by an hour. Their mother liked to say that Jules had been a natural homebody and preferred to stay in the familiar fixtures of her mom's belly.

"Romey -no. Stop that.” Jules brushed her sister’s probing hands away from her body. “I’m fine. In fact, I'm better than fine."

Jules took a deep breath, drawing out the moment. It was a big announcement she was about to make. The biggest admission of her life. It needed the dramatic pause.

“I...am...” Jules took another deep breath, letting go of the last two words with a wondrous sigh. “In love."

Romey's expression didn’t change. Her gaze still roamed over her twin as though she were looking for a bruise, a cut, some sort of wound. Finally, she inhaled and then let out a sigh of her own.

"Well, good,” Romey said. “I knew that's what you wanted. If you've realized that you can love Paris, all the better."

"No, no, Romey.” Jules held up her hands, waving them to ward off such a notion. “I’m not in love with Paris."

“Then I don’t understand? I don't see how you're going to marry Paris if you think you're in love with someone else? You haven’t shown interest in any other man on the commune.”

“He’s not from the commune,” Jules admitted. "We just met."

“Today?” asked Romey.

Jules nodded.

“Here?” Romey pointed to the patch of dirt beneath their feet.

Jules bit her lip but gave her sister another nod.

Romey regarded her twin for a long moment. Jules could see the wheels turning in her sister's head. While Jules had stayed behind to luxuriate in their mother's belly for that hour, Romey had taken the head start to get the lay of the land. Those additional sixty minutes gave Romey the false sense that she was wiser than her younger sister.

"I think these oils and sugary scents are getting to you," said Romey. "You're not making any sense."

Jules knew better than to try to speak emotions with her science-minded sister. She had to use logic. Although logic didn't actually apply in this matter because Jules had fallen in love, head over heels in love, with a man she'd only just met. A man she didn't know much of anything about.

Except that his name was David. And that his friends were cruel for calling him Porco. Even though pigs were delightful creatures and smart too. as evidenced by her pet pig Hamlet who could always track her down no matter where she was on the commune. Jules bet David was just as smart and loyal as a pig.

But that was all she knew about him. That and that he'd dated Rosalind. And possibly another girl... or two. Or more...

But none of that mattered. What mattered was what she'd felt between them. That had been real.

"Who is this man?" said Romey.

"His name is David."

"David what?"

“I... I um... don't know his last name...yet."

Romey raised a brow. Though they were twins, Jules had never mastered the raise of one eyebrow. Or the lowering of it.

“Okay,” Romey said. “What does he do?"

“I, um...” Jules huffed in frustration. Trust her practical sister to ruin it. “Romey, we just met."

"And now what?" her sister asked.

"I don't know? All I know is that he made my heart skip a beat. That's never happened with Paris. That's never happened with any guy I've know.”

"But you're in love?” Romey was using her logical voice. The voice that went *if this then that must follow*. “If you're heart skips, then love must follow, right?”

Well, it didn't sound wrong. Before Jules could respond, Romey kept treading down her logic trail.

“What you experienced was likely a heart palpitation, which happens during exercise, heat, or even low blood sugar. It's hot out here, so you're likely overheated. Have you eaten?”

“What? Um... no, not since breakfast.”

"And you've been walking, in the heat, with no food in your belly. So, you see, it's not love. It's your body crying for shade, water, and sustenance."

Jules seethed. How had the two of them shared a womb? How, in fact, did they share the same DNA when they saw the world so differently?

"This is why I didn't want to tell you," said Jules.

"Paris is a smart decision," Romey said. "Don't throw your life away on misfiring synapses. All over a man you just met and know nothing about."

Romey reached out to rub Jules's shoulder. The wound wasn't there, her sister had plucked at the center of Jules's heart. Misfired synapses or not, Jules was determined to find David and see what would follow.

She wouldn't get that chance at this moment. Paris was headed toward her. Just as he took his first step in her direction, his gaze shifted. A dark cloud passed over his features as he watched a woman walk down the cleared path of the fair.

Brenda Vance walked past the commune's booth. In both hands, she held leads. Tethered to the ends of each lead was a young calf. Children trailed after the female rancher, unaware that those innocent animals would one day reach their maturity and then be led to slaughter.

Jules wasn't a fool. She knew that was the natural order of things. She simply chose to get her sustenance a different way, the same way the cows did. From the fields.

What upset her was that the Vances tainted those fields with harsh, unnatural chemicals.

As she walked by with her calves and parade of children, Brenda glanced over at the booth finding Paris. Jules held her breath as the generations-old enemies glared at one another. Unlike their fathers who had come to blows, Paris and Brenda only threw daggers with their eyes. That and the legal paperwork each of their lawyers had filed, bound both their hands. The agreement of when, where, and what chemicals could be sprayed had kept the peace so far. But that peace was as tenuous as the thin boundary connecting their lands.

Brenda gave a nod of her head, her eyes ever watchful. Paris deigned to do the same. But it was clear that a line had been drawn in the sand between the two lands. Jules stood firmly behind her family on the commune, the place she'd lived all her life, where she drew her sustenance as well as her livelihood.

There were only two Vances remaining. Brenda's brother was one of the town's pastors. His efforts had lent a huge hand in keeping the peace between the families. Brenda had recently married a soldier, and now she had a small army on her side. A group of tall, well-formed men flanked the cattle rancher. Jules's heart skipped another few beats when she recognized the face of one man in particular.

She'd only seen his shaggy brown hair once, but she'd have easily picked him out of a crowd. She'd been under the direct assault of that grin only moments ago. Seeing it again made her stagger a footstep back now. She took another step back as David's grin slowly fell.

Recognition dawned in his dark eyes as their gazes locked. Happiness, confusion, awe, denial all lit his face at once. Jules had the urge to shield her gaze from the onslaught of his emotions. She didn't get the chance to.

Paris stepped in front of her, blocking her view of David. Jules shifted to catch another glimpse of him. Her heartbeat tripped over itself as she realized they were looking at each other from across an imaginary line in the sand.

## CHAPTER NINE

Porco stutter-stepped when he saw her, feeling that same draw to run to her and scoop her into his arms. But something had held him back. First, it was Spinelli's grip on his arm. Then the tilt of his head and raise of his eyebrow that told Porco he was missing something.

Yeah, he was missing something. The feel of his woman against him. The touch of her cheek to his. The taste of her lips on his tongue. But there was something he wasn't seeing.

As Porco walked by with his friends, he noted that the people around Jules glared at them. Which was odd. They were all dressed in bright, colorful clothing that harkened back to the sixties and seventies. They looked like they'd stepped out of a history book carrying a banner that said *We are flower children.*

Though that's not what the sign above them said. It read Verona Commune Organic Vegan Produce and Goods. Porco's mind worked hard to comprehend the significance of the sign blaring overhead. It was difficult because his gaze kept returning to Jules. His entire being insisted that he go to her, claim her, make her his in every way. He just needed to figure out what he was missing.

Was it the word organic that should hold his attention? He knew that that was a buzz word touted in the health and fitness industry. All he knew was that when something was labeled organic in the grocery store, it came with a hefty price tag.

There was that word vegan again. It couldn't have anything to do with race. There were people behind those tables of every skin tone. Which meant Porco owed Spinelli and Rusty an apology for calling them racist.

But he had heard that term before? Oh, he remembered. He'd been on the market for a new leather jacket and saw a cheaper model called vegan leather. Was that it?

No. There was something bigger he was missing.

"That's her, isn't it?" said Spinelli.

Porco couldn't speak. He could only gaze at Jules. She was staring back at him. Unlike earlier, her eyes didn't sparkle as she looked at him. Neither was she smiling shyly. Her gaze was clouded and she worried her lip with her teeth.

Something was wrong. So why wasn't he moving towards her? Oh, because Spinelli still held him back.

"Do you see what I mean now?" asked Spinelli.

See what? All Porco saw was the woman, who was very likely to be the mother of his children, standing in a small crowd of colorfully dressed people... who were also frowning and glaring at his group. What was he missing?

A man stepped in front of Jules. He was tall with dark hair. His body was lean, with the type of muscle that Porco had seen on yoga instructors. Porco doubted the man could bench more than fifty pounds if that. Still, the yogi had placed himself between Porco and Porco's woman. That would not do.

"No, no. You can't go there." Spinelli's grip tightened on Porco's arm.

Jordan Spinelli had a big brain and a big body to match. His grip was absolute. But Porco was not above sucker punching his friend if both he and the yogini stood in the way of true love.

"You cannot go over there," Spinelli continued. "Because of the lawsuit."

Lawsuit? What was Spinelli talking about? Porco's brain whirled as realization began to dawn. Hadn't he heard Brenda and her brother going on about a dispute with the neighbors?

"The Verona Commune filed an injunction dictating where and what type of chemicals Brenda could spray on her lands."

Porco did remember that. Vaguely. Something or other about fertilizer and vegetables. He thought maybe the term organic had been used in that conversation.

"That's them," said Spinelli. "That's the Verona Commune."

Here he was, staring down the neighbors from hell. Meanwhile, all Porco could think was that he'd been right next to Jules for months and had been unaware. Oh, fate was a tricky little devil.

"That's why it can't work out between you two. Well, that's one of many reasons."

Spinelli's words made no sense. Porco had no bone in this fight. This was between Brenda, and the leader, who Porco now assumed was the tree standing posed yoga instructor.

This feud had nothing to do with him and Jules. Or what they were feeling towards each other. Right?

Porco looked again to the woman of his dreams. Jules's eyes were squeezed closed, as though she was trying to shut out the same realization he'd just come to. She had to know that he wasn't a part of what was going on between Brenda and Mini Mountain Pose guy.

Jules opened her eyes. Her gaze immediately fell on Porco. What he saw in her brown depths made him believe. There was a spark of hope. It was all he needed to do the impossible.

As part of the Army's premier raid force, Porco had been on numerous missions where he'd infiltrated hostile territory. He'd spent weekends tracking enemy combatants and pulling terrorists out of their beds before their eyes blinked open. He'd run headfirst into dark caves and decrepit cities to rescue prisoners of war and innocent civilians.

Each and every one of those missions had spiked his adrenalin, engaged his flight or fight responses, and made him question his sanity. One thing remained the same every time; he'd never hesitated to take that first step into combat.

But here, in this sedate Montana town, where the biggest threat was the fried oil dough and meats the townsfolk launched at their livers and hearts, Porco faced his toughest battle. He ignored all his training to run headfirst. He turned off his fight response and kept moving forward.

Walking past Jules Capulano had to be the hardest thing Porco had done in his life. But he did it. Because he had the hope that she would meet him tonight as planned. Outside of the scrutiny of their feuding families, away from the lawsuit that tied up their lands, out of the boundaries of who others thought they should date.

With that knowledge, Porco soldiered on. He marched away from the woman who was made for him. With this mission of losing this first battle accomplished, Porco began plotting how to win the war.

# CHAPTER TEN

"The nerve of that woman." Paris paced the length of the field. The sun was setting, and the light low. However, his stomping feet never smashed into a single gourd or tomato. The fruits of his labors were always handled with the utmost care and respect. "Did you see her? Parading those poor animals around like that."

"I believe she'd set up a petting zoo for the children at the other end of the fair," Jules said, trying to play peacemaker in a war she'd never wanted in on.

She was surprised the role had landed at her feet. It usually went to Paris, especially while his father had been alive. Now, Jules saw flashes of the fiery Heathcliff in his gentle son.

"That's another thing," Paris went on as though he hadn't heard Jules's tone, which was also unlike him. Paris was one of the most attentive and intuitive people she'd ever met. "Putting those poor babies on display like they were some exhibit."

In addition to being an advocate for clean living and eating, Paris was also an animal rights activist. Though unlike his father, Paris's activism had always tended towards the letter-writing and sign-making campaigns. Whenever anyone had a conflict on the commune, Paris insisted they write out their problems and put them in the Problem Jar. After reading the grievances, disagreeing residents had to come into an Empathy Circle where they would hug it out. That's how problems got solved here. This was the first time Jules had ever seen a hint of violence in his eyes.

"And to put those soldiers on display like that. Did you see them?"

Oh, yes, Jules had seen them. One in particular. It had taken everything in her to not run up to David and wrap her arms around him. The pull towards the man was maddening, unlike anything she'd ever felt.

She'd hated being across a divide from him when she knew in her soul that they should be walking beside each other, hand in hand, fingers twined, hearts matching the same beat. When David had frowned at her across that imaginary line in the sand, Jules had feared it was all over for them before it had even begun.

How could this ever work? He was one of the soldiers staying and working at the Vance Ranch. Her loyalties were to the people of the commune, her family, and friends. The line separating them wasn't imaginary. It was real. That fenced-in border was not to be crossed. There was a legal document that said so.

She'd seen the look of utter dejection on David's face. Jules had felt the same. They'd both touched starlight, only later to feel the burn.

But then, something miraculous happened. The twinkle came back into David's eyes. His chin lifted in defiance, rising higher than that imaginary line in the ground. Higher even than the border that separated them. The look in his eyes told Jules that he still wanted her. The feeling in her heart told her that she wanted the same.

Could this even work? Could she still go to him tonight? Would it mean she was betraying her people if she did? She knew that it would be a betrayal of her heart if she didn't.

"Those soldiers are nothing but mindless, brainwashed automatons," Paris was saying. His pacing doing the work of a trough in the rich soil.

"I heard that the soldiers of the Purple Heart Ranch have been doing a lot of community service work, especially with the youth," said Jules.

"They're convincing children to enlist and become drones like them."

Jules had nothing against the military. Her grandfather had been one of the famed Tuskegee Airmen. Though her father had no designs on service himself, he proudly displayed his father's accomplishments in his home.

"This is so unlike you," she said to Paris. "Why are you so upset?"

Paris took a deep inhale. He let out the air in a long, intoned *Om* as they'd been taught as children. Jules waited patiently until the man got control of himself. She couldn't ever remember seeing him this upset. To say that Paris Montgomery was mild-mannered was an understatement.

"I'm sorry," he said, reaching for her hands. "I'm just stressed. We have a lot riding on this inspection, our entire future."

Jules stared down at their joined hands. When David had held her hands in his, she'd felt a fire ignite inside of her. Paris's hands weren't cold. They were rough, callused from his daily work in the fields. She appreciated everything his hands had done for her over the years. When her parents had passed away, Paris had been there, steady as ever to help them through it. She'd found comfort when he'd held her hands back then. She'd found solace in his arms when he'd offered his shoulder to cry on.

Paris was a good man. A good friend. But he did not light any kind of fire in her.

"Speaking of the future, there's something I've been meaning to talk to you about." Paris chewed at his inner lip. He always did that when he was unsure of himself.

The part of Jules that was this man's friend rose to the fore. She wanted to offer him comfort, even in this. As a reflex, she gave his hands a squeeze. It was the wrong move. She could see the courage gather in his eyes. He opened his mouth to speak and—

"Oink."

Hamlet situated his big body between the two of them, knocking their hands apart. Jules could kiss the pig. In fact, she leaned down and gave his scruffy head a rub of thanks.

“I should probably get him in his pen for the night,” she said.

“We’ll talk about this later?”

Jules nodded, already leading the pig away. She made quick strides towards the home she shared with her sister. Hamlet kept up on his stubby legs and excess weight.

In the distance, Jules saw the light of the nightly bonfire. Each night her people came together, be it in the communal hall if the weather was poor, or out under the stars. They broke bread, shared anecdotes of their day, told stories of the past, discussed their hopes for the future.

Jules had her own hopes for the future. She just hoped that what she planned to do, and whom she planned to do it with, wouldn’t bar her from her seat at the communes table moving forward.

## CHAPTER ELEVEN

She came.

Until he saw her walking through the crowd, Porco had doubted. Not what he felt for her. Not the connection he knew existed between them. But he knew that family was a powerful motivator. If Jules's family was not on board with her seeing him, she might've stayed home.

But she came.

As first dates went, this one wasn't so bad. Porco walked alongside Jules amidst the sounds of the county fair. The wails, screeches, and cries of children who were finally coming down from their afternoon sugar rush. The shouts and giggles of teens testing the boundaries of their independence while inside the cocoon of their tight-knit community were now on the rise. Ever-present was the catcalls of the visiting vendors aiming to pick the last dollar out of eager townies' pockets.

"You hungry?" Porco asked.

Jules tugged at the hem of her sleeve. She'd changed from the brightly colored sundress she'd worn this morning to more muted tones. The dress she now wore was white cloth. There were a few accents of light blue and purple at the sleeve and hem. The softness of the colors cast her in an ethereal glow, making her look like more of the angel in his dreams.

"I ate before I left home," she said. "Most of the foods here don't agree with me."

Right. The vegan thing. No meat.

"We could have a milkshake if you're thirsty."

She tugged again at the blue trim on her sleeve. She'd met his eyes only once, that moment when they'd come face to face for the first time tonight. She'd said hello, gazing into Porco's eyes as if searching for something. Only when she found it, her features had gone pensive, like she was now working out a complex math problem.

"I can't have dairy," she said finally.

"Oh. Well, there's also ice cream."

She found his gaze then. Her eyes sparkled in

the moonlight. He felt that he was now the complex math problem she was trying to work out. Porco wanted to tell her that he was a very simple solution.

“We’re on a date,” he said. “I want to buy you a treat. Is there anything I can get for you?”

Jules pressed her lips together. She glanced up, eyes searching the signs and boards around them. “Well," she said, "Oreos are vegan."

There was that word again. Porco supposed he should ask her exactly what it meant. But he didn't want to offend her or seem stupid. He'd google it later tonight after their date. Though the thought of leaving her at any point didn't sit well with him. This date had only begun, and he wanted it to go on forever.

He watched as she took a tentative bite of the dessert. It wasn’t a regular Oreo from a package. It had been covered in batter and deep-fried in oil. Jules’s eyes went wide. Her hand went to her head.

"Sugar rush," she said through a wince. “That’s more sugar than I’m used to... in a week.“

Porco placed his hand over hers, rubbing at her temple. Jules dropped her hands and gave him complete control over her head. Porco had never felt stronger than when he was given charge of this woman.

He massaged the skin at her forehead. His hands cupped her cheek. He gazed down at her, unabashed. He watched the tension slowly seep from her. When she opened her eyes, the golden sparkles there dazzled him.

Porco's heart raced. With his fingers grazing her neck, he felt her pulse pick up. Her breaths came out in quick huffs. He tasted a sweetness that transcended the sugars of the cookie. There was a smear of frosting at the corner of her upper lip. He should bend down to lick that off. Wouldn't want her to experience another rush from the sugar.

Was it too soon? Funny, he'd never asked himself that question before when pursuing a woman. Jules was different. He wanted -no needed to get this one right. She was different. She was special. She was The One.

"You've got something there," he said.

Carefully, he brushed the spot at the corner of her mouth. Grabbing a napkin from a nearby dispenser, he handed the paper cloth to her. As she busied herself wiping at her lips, Porco turned and snuck a lick of his thumb.

Heaven.

"It's funny," he said, as they walked on. "Most first

dates take place at a bar after meeting on a dating app."

"Why is that funny?" she asked.

He turned to her, taking a moment when his heart leaped at the sight of her. It hadn't stopped doing that all night. It would probably weaken with all the exertion just being in her presence. It would be worth it.

"We met naturally," he said. "You don't hear a lot of stories of people doing that. Well, except on the Purple Heart Ranch and Vance Ranch. But those are all special cases."

Jules winced at the mention of the ranch. Porco wanted to bite his tongue. They had seemed to mutually agree to keep the subject of their feuding ranches off the table.

"I don't have a cell phone," said Jules. "So, I don't have any apps."

"No cell phone?"

She shrugged. "I live on the commune. Everyone I want to talk to is in shouting distance. Don't look at me like I'm from outer space."

She poked him in the side with her elbow. He had her talking now, relaxed. The more her guard came down, the more he got to know about her. The more he got to know about her, the more he liked her.

"We have a few computers and the internet for work purposes in the community room. But no television."

He blanched at the thought. No phones or television? He wouldn't survive. Except, he had lived like that for stretches of time.

"We didn't always have creature comforts in the army. But if we were at a base, there might be access. Even in the desert or the mountains, many soldiers were able to take college courses or other training between missions."

"All the places you got to see." Jules tilted her head back and sighed. Her gaze was fixed on the stars.

"Do you want to travel?" he asked.

She gave a shake of her head. "I used to think I did. I realized I like the idea of traveling. But everything I need is here. My family, my friends, my work."

"What is your work?"

"I grow soybeans."

Porco wrinkled his nose.

"You don't like beans?"

"Not when I was a kid, no. But I'm willing to give

them another try if they're your beans."

Again, her gaze clouded. He'd become a math problem again. More than anything, Porco wanted to add up to her needs.

"Do you know anything about me?" she asked. "About my people and where I come from?"

He didn't know much about the next-door neighbors on the Verona Commune. They were farmers like most who lived in these parts. He'd heard lively music once or twice as he'd driven by; ancient, primal sounds with drums beating and tambourines jingling. It had sounded like a good time. If these were modern-day flower children, he figured he'd have a good time with them. Right now, he was entirely focused on having a good time with the bloom beside him.

"I probably shouldn't be here with you," she said. But her words were whispered, quietly. So softly that they would've easily been lost in the sound of revelry all around them.

"But you are," he said.

Jules worried the hem of her sleeve even more. Porco reached for those slender fingers. Uncoupling them from the fabric, he slid the fingers of his left hand between the fingers of her right one. Not quite down to the knuckle, just to the first line past her fingertips.

"You're here with me."

In her eyes, Porco saw the plusses and minuses of the problem she'd been trying to solve fall away. He slid his fingers down past her knuckles.

"It's what we both want."

With that, Porco let their hands clasp fully. He grasped onto the webbing between her fingers. His palm met hers, giving him another rush of heat that pulsed all through his body. His heart warned him to hold onto this one tight and never let go. Those were instructions Porco intended to follow to the letter.

## CHAPTER TWELVE

If she reached up, Jules swore she could touch the stars. She was flying high. Luckily, she was strapped in with a seat belt.

The Ferris wheel rose her and David up higher and higher until the world below appeared small as a puzzle board whose pieces she no longer cared to fit in each space. She was beyond that, above it, making a new picture, playing a new game.

Her heart raced with her feet having left the ground. Her palms were slick with anticipation. Her breaths came in short pants. Beside her, David still held her hand.

Jules had never felt so exhilarated before. She was wide awake but felt like she was moving through a dream. Her thoughts were scattered, but everything made perfect sense. This was exactly where she was meant to be, at this elevation, at this moment, with this man.

Turning to look at her companion, she saw that David wasn't looking at the stars. He was gazing at her. As though she were the brightest thing in the sky. She would never tire of being the focal point of his attention.

"Tell me everything about you," he said.

Jules had never had anyone ask her that. Back home, everyone already knew everything about her. They'd all been there when anything happened. But here was a person who knew nothing about her. She could tell him anything. She could be whoever she wanted to be. All she wanted David to know was the truth of her, who she was down in her core. She wanted him to know and like that person.

"I'm a twin."

The corners of his lips lifted into a delighted grin. "There's two of you."

"No," she chuckled. "Not exactly. Romey and I are very different creatures. She's entirely sensible, where my head is often in the clouds."

David chuckled. "Sounds like my friend Spinelli. He's always telling me to come back down to earth."

"Romey speaks to me in conditional statements."

Jules let her voice go more nasally in the know-it-all pitch of her sister, "'Jules, if your head is in the clouds, then you would drown because clouds are made of water'."

"I've got one for you." David lifted his chin higher as though taking on a superior air. "'Porco, love is nothing more than a spasm of the heart valves, which amounts to nothing more than a medical condition'."

"Romey's said that!"

David's chuckle mixed with her giggles. Their glee sounded like the perfect harmony. When next she looked over, Jules noted that they sat even closer together than before.

Her soldier's gaze dipped to her lips. Jules's breath caught. Though she didn't watch television or movies, she read her fair share of books. She'd read about what couples got up to on this particular ride. This high up away from prying eyes was the perfect opportunity for kissing.

But he didn't.

"Tell me more," he said.

Jules swallowed, taking a moment to find her voice and hide her disappointment.

"My parents met at the end of the Civil Rights Movement. All of the marches were over. They'd missed a lot of the action. My mother had tried to join the Black Panther Party, but they weren't accepting white women."

Jules grinned, thinking about her fierce, activist mother. Mariam Capulano always marched at the front of the lines wherever she saw injustice meted out. It didn't matter that she had barely been five feet tall and one hundred pounds only after a Sunday potluck. If she saw an underdog, she was immediately on their side.

"My father was a literary historian. He loved Shakespeare, hence our names; Jules and Romey."

David's grin grew wider. His thumb rubbed lazy circles at the center of her palm. He'd turned his body towards her, giving her his full, undivided, fascinated attention.

"They had us later in life. Instead of raising us in the city, they founded the commune along with the Montgomerys. They wanted to create an idyllic setting where racial and cultural harmony reigned. They both passed away a few years ago."

"I'm sorry."

Her mother had gone first. Her father lost the will to live shortly after burying his wife.

"Anyway, I grew up on the land they bought for

us. I have a knack for making things grow. I haven't really done much else. I haven't even dated."

"Really?"

"I grew up with all the boys on the commune. They're like brothers to me. So, I waited."

"Now, I'm here."

David lifted the back of her hand and kissed it. Warmth shot all the way through her. A voice that sang from her blood began chanting, *Yes, this one.*

With the voices in her head and the warmth stretching to every extremity, Jules couldn't think of a thing to say. All she could do was hold onto this man beside her she barely knew but felt like home.

They stayed like that for another cycle of the Ferris wheel. Up and down and around they went. All the while, David held her hand, and her gaze. It didn't feel like staring. It felt like unwrapping the present she'd wanted her entire life.

"It's your turn," she said on the way back up. "Tell me about you."

"I grew up in a big city. Lots of people. I wasn't great at school. Was diagnosed with ADHD. Counselors pointed me to the Army. It was the best thing that ever happened to me. Turned out all I needed was a bit of structure and discipline. Joining the Army Rangers gave me a purpose, something to fight for."

Jules remembered Paris's disdain of the military. He'd been certain that the organization brainwashed individuals. Taking lives to further some hidden agenda.

That hadn't been the case with her grandfather and the mission of the Tuskegee Airmen. Those brave souls had protected people across the globe from a reign of tyranny during the second world war. Now she saw that the army had helped shape the path of the man her heart cried out to. If he hadn't become a soldier, would he have found his way to a ranch in the middle of Montana where soldiers came to heal?

"Now that that life is over, I've opened a training camp with my friends." David grinned, as if at a private joke. "Now I'm the discipliner."

He never seemed to take himself seriously. Jules really liked that about him. She'd grown up around men who debated policy, politics, and philosophy all day, every day. There was nothing heavy about David. He liked to laugh at himself and the world.

"Jules, I need you to know something about me."

"Yes, David?" She leaned in closer. She wanted to know everything about him.

"I've been on a lot of dates. Because I've been looking for The One."

The way he said The One sent shivers along her arms. The hairs at the back of her neck stood at attention, waiting for his command.

“I want you to know that I don't plan to go on any more dates."

Jules had no idea what he meant. She was too busy watching his lips form words. His voice was so silky, like the petals of a new bean sprout.

"This is the last one?" she asked.

"This is my last date. With you."

Her mind raced in the opposite direction of what he meant. The reason she knew it was the opposite direction of where David was trying to go was because as her mind zigged to thinking that he didn't care to pursue anything with her, David was leaning into her.

The first brush of his lips woke something inside of her. She felt like a seedling pushing through the warm earth. Every seed knew it needed to fight hard to get to the top of the soil. Only when it broke free of the earth would it find its true form of sustenance, sunlight.

David's kiss was like the first ray of sunlight. Jules felt herself unfurling for him. She stretched her limbs towards him. She tilted her bulbous head back to drink in more of him. But he pulled away from her, taking his life-giving light with him.

"Tell me you feel it too," he whispered against her lips.

She didn't need to ask him what he meant. It was there burning bright between them. "The spark."

"Tell me I'm the one for you."

Did he really need the words? Couldn't he hear it in her breath, in her blood, in the erratic thumping of her heart?

"Yes, David. I'm yours," she said. "I never want this to end."

# CHAPTER THIRTEEN

Porco hadn't attended church much while he'd been living here in Montana. His mother had been a social butterfly in her congregation. So much so that Porco knew that the best places for hiding were the vestry and the loft. Only new friends would hide in the sacristy and get found immediately.

While Porco went to church to play, his dad only went to the hallowed halls because a day without his wife was unfathomable. While Jane Porco raised her voiced in the choir, Daniel Porco kept his gaze fastened on her. Their son spent his time between watching the bright light of love that passed between his parents and keeping an eye out for any girl that might look at him in the same way.

Plenty of the girls that came to church smiled Porco's way, and he always smiled back. How could he not? He loved to gaze at the opposite sex, wondering if the next one might be The One. They were all pretty, dressed in their Sunday best. Even today, the sight of shiny Mary Janes set his heart beating.

Jules wasn't wearing Mary Janes as they stepped into the town's church. She had on Birkenstock sandals. Her toenails were painted a deep purple, her heels had a dusting of dirt from the walk through the fairgrounds to the church.

Though her footwear wasn't shiny and new, Porco still felt the thrill from his Sundays prowling the pews. He opened the doors of the church for Jules, knowing he'd never need to search a nave again. He'd found The One.

"Is that you, Porco?" Pastor Walter Vance stood at the pulpit, arranging papers. The tall man looked like he belonged on the back of a horse and not in a sanctuary. He'd been raised on the cattle ranch. Though he'd done his chores every day alongside his sister, Walter had felt pulled for a different calling, as evidenced by the white-collar at his neck.

"You finally hear the voice of God and come to repent all your sins?" Pastor Vance asked with a smile in his voice. The smile dropped when he saw Jules beside Porco. "Ms. Capulano?"

Vance looked between the two of them. His congenial expression moving from friendly, to confused. Then darkening with comprehension and finally crumbling into disdain.

"Oh, no," moaned Vance. "No. No. No." He wagged his finger at them as though they were naughty children. "You cannot ask me to do this."

"We want to get married," Porco proclaimed proudly.

The pastor's shoulders slumped down along with his crumpled features. Porco couldn't understand why? This shouldn't come as a surprise. Everyone in his unit was married. Only he and Spinelli remained. And Porco doubted Spinelli would ever walk down the aisle unless there was the answer to a math problem at the end of it.

Aside from that, Porco had had numerous conversations with the pastor about his desire to find the right woman and settle down. Though he did remember Vance going on about something to do with quality over quantity. Porco couldn't remember the exact details of the conversation because a pretty woman had been walking by. Had he dated her? Or maybe he'd dated the friend she'd been walking with?

None of that mattered. Jules was on his arm. Her warmth danced along his skin until it infused itself in his body. If she wasn't already, she would soon be a part of him. He might've had a lot of dates over his lifetime. All those experiences were what let him know that he'd finally found the right one.

Jules was pure quality. Nothing could be higher. He wanted to spend the rest of his life with her. She'd agreed to do the same with him.

"Do you know who she is?" said Vance, jerking his thumb at Jules. Before Porco could answer, the pastor turned to Jules, his thumb switched direction. "Do you know who he is?"

"He's the man I want to spend the rest of my life with," was her answer.

Porco felt his heart thumping in his chest. It stuttered, making a *ba-bump* sound instead of its normal thump. All too soon he realized, it wasn't just his heart he heard beating. It was her heart too.

He squeezed her hand. He couldn't wait to kiss each digit. Then he would take her lips again.

"How did the two of you even meet?" asked Pastor Vance. Again, before either could answer, he held up his hands like a stop sign. "Don't tell me.

You climbed the boundary fence to get to her like something out of *Romeo and Juliet*. Because that's what this is. Your two ranches are feuding."

"But we're not feuding," said Porco. He gazed down at Jules. The same light of adoration shone from her hazel eyes. "I believe everyone will come around when they see how we feel about each other."

That stopped the pastor in his tracks. Though Porco hadn't been paying much attention to the problems between the Vance Ranch and the Verona Commune, he knew that Brenda's brother had acted as the go-between for the two sides. This marriage could be the tie that knotted the two lands together.

"How long has this been going on?" asked Vance.

"We met this morning," said Porco.

Vance sighed, pinching the bridge of his nose. He clutched his Bible to his chest and looked heavenward. His features appeared pensive, as though he was asking the Lord *Why me?*

"Pastor Vance," said Jules, "I know this might seem sudden."

"No, you two aren't the record," he said. "My sister and Keaton only knew each other a few hours before saying their vows. By that math, you two have been dating for a couple of months."

"Then why are you hesitating?" said Porco.

"Because the Keatons and the Vances weren't involved in a generations-old feud," said Vance.

"This feud is between your sister and Paris," said Jules. "The two of them need to work it out. David and I know what we want, and that is each other."

Such elegant words from those perfect lips. If Vance wouldn't marry them, Porco would drive them to Vegas tonight. There would be nothing to keep him from this woman.

"You want to spend the rest of your life with this man," said the pastor, "and all it entails?"

Jules nodded her head. "We'll weather whatever may come."

Pastor Vance turned to Porco. Before he could utter a word, Porco answered him.

"Whatever may come."

"My sister and Keaton with the prenup, I knew what to do there. Patty and Grizz with their unrequited love, easy. Mac and Lana practically married themselves. This one..." Pastor Vance motioned to Jules and Porco's joined hands. "...this one I did not see coming."

The pastor dropped his head. His gaze focused on the Bible in his hands. His thumb pressed on the golden-foiled edges of the pages causing them to flip rapidly under his fingers. As his thumb came to the end of the book, his eyes lit. He looked up at Jules and Porco as though inspiration had struck without reading a single word from the good book.

"I suppose I should offer a bit of premarital counseling," he said, his tone was a mockery of somberness. "You both understand that there are certain expectations in a marriage. There are roles that you must take on."

"Both our parents stayed married until death," said Porco. "We had good role models. Both my mother and father worked and took care of the kids."

"Mine, too," said Jules.

Another thing they had in common. There was so much to learn about this woman. They had a lifetime to tell each other every story and share many more.

Pastor Vance pinched at his lower lip. "What about financial roles?"

"We're both gainfully employed," said Porco. "Jules grows organ beans."

"Organic soybeans," she corrected.

"Right," said Porco. "The bottom line is we both run our own profitable businesses."

Vance pinched at his strong, square jaw. "Okay, how will you resolve conflicts?"

"I feel like I can tell him anything," said Jules. "We already understand each other."

"And if we have a problem we can't solve," said Porco, "we'll just come to you."

The pastor didn't appear to find that funny at all. He cleared his throat, giving his collar a tug. "What about the marital bed?"

Porco felt a rush of heat run through him. His palms warmed where he held her hand in his. Jules was inexperienced. This was her first date. He'd given her her first kiss.

"I'll wait," said Porco. This marriage might be rushed, but he would not rush her into anything.

"Actually," said Jules, tugging shyly at her lower lip, "I'm ready."

"Let's get on with it." Porco had to swallow a few times before he got the words out. He faced the pastor squarely, done with the man's stalling tactics. This marriage was moving forward. Now.

"One more thing," said the pastor. "Where will you live?"

Porco hadn't thought of that. He was staying in one of the ranch hand bunks on Brenda's land. His roommates were Spinelli and Rusty. Not exactly the best situation for newlyweds.

"We'll stay on my farm," said Jules. "My sister and I have our own cabin there."

That worked for Porco. He'd never been a stickler for where he laid his head at night. As long as he'd get to lay it next to Jules, he would not complain.

"You do realize your families will fight this?" Once again, Pastor Vance's shoulders deflated in defeat. But his sigh had a note of hope as it escaped his mouth.

"Or they'll come together when they see that we're in love," said Jules.

# CHAPTER FOURTEEN

This was really happening, just like in her dreams. Only this was better.

Jules had never dreamed that her dream man would be so handsome. That his hands would be so soft and firm at the same time. That simply standing next to him would make her feel both powerful and docile at the same time.

She felt a twinge of guilt that her sister wasn't here to witness this. They'd done everything together since they were born. But there had been that hour where Romey had gotten a head start on her. And there was also the possibility that sensible Romey would've tried to talk her sixty-minute-younger-sibling out of this. And there was no way Jules wasn't going forward with this.

"They say that sometimes opposites attract," said Pastor Vance. "I think the reality is that the two forces weren't as opposite as once was initially believed."

He leaned against the pulpit, looking out of the window at the night's sky rather at the two of them. Jules wasn't entirely sure the man was still aware of their presence.

This was Jules's first time in the church. She was far from an atheist. At a young age, her parents had given her and her sister a stack of holy books. Part of their homeschooling was to read them all and make their own decisions. The project included papers, presentations, and a test at the end. Romey's final answer was that God was found in the perfection of nature, while Jules declared that God was love.

"I've found that the happiest couples are rarely the same to outward appearances," Pastor Vance was still philosophizing. Or was he preaching? He might've started the proceedings to marry them. "They are the same on the inside, and that's where you find that you best understand each other's differences."

Outwardly, she and David did appear different. He was a soldier. She was a modern-day flower child. But they'd looked past those differences to the heart of one another and felt an intense attraction.

"Your families are opposites," said Pastor Vance. "Like magnets giving off two negative forces, they repel. But the two of you have turned around and looked at one another to see a different side."

Yes, that was it. They were like magnets. Drawn together, no matter which way you turned them.

David smiled down at her. Like the magnets they were accused of being, he took her hand in his. Jules felt that warmth of electricity zing across her fingertips.

"God is the spark. He's put you two in each other's paths to do His work. I am His servant. Though Lord, I hope you will protect me from my sister."

Once again, Pastor Vance looked up at the ceiling. He let out a long, weary exhale and then made a sign of the cross over his chest. Returning his attention to the couple before him, he gave first Jules and then David a thoughtful gaze. Finally, his face broke into the congenial grin he was known for.

"And now for the vows."

"Wait," said David. "I have something to say first."

Jules's heart skipped a beat. A fluttery feeling

crept into her stomach, and she tingled all over. Was he backing out?

"Jules, I know this is crazy; what we're doing. But something in me recognizes you as my home, as my shelter. My mom told me that when I found The One, I'd know it because I'd feel a spark. That's not what I felt with you."

Jules lost her breath. He was breaking up with her. Her first date, her first kiss, her first marriage, and her first break up all on the same day. So why was David clutching her hands tightly, like he planned to never let go?

"It wasn't a spark like my mom said. It was an explosion. It rocked my world. I know I'm not thinking straight, but I don't have a single doubt that this is the right thing to do. I'm not a perfect man, but I know that you are perfect for me."

Jules let out a shaky breath as she regarded this man. Neither had said the word, but she felt it humming between them. That spark, that explosion, that feeling, it could be nothing but love.

True love.

"David, being with you is the most natural thing in the world to me. What's between us, that spark we feel, it's like a seed. I've put it in my heart, and you've put it in yours. We'll grow it with our care and attention. We'll nurture it with time and patience. It will grow strong, and it will feed everyone we love and care about, and then they'll see... they'll see that what we feel is real. It's natural. It's... everything."

David looked down at her with eyes shining so bright that she felt warmed through. She had only kissed him once. Right now, she wanted to do it again. She wanted to do it forever. And very soon, she could.

"Those were perfect vows if ever I heard them," said Pastor Vance. "Julia Starflower Capulano—"

A snort escaped David's mouth, which he promptly covered, only to chuckle again. "Starflower? Your middle name is Starflower?"

"Yes." Jules lifted her chin. "My parents let me pick my own middle name when I was five. What of it?"

David's face sobered. "Nothing. It's beautiful." He winced as though trying to keep an errant chuckle down. Lucky for him, he succeeded.

"Julia, do you take this man to be your lawful wedded husband?"

Jules let go of her annoyance and answered honestly, with all her heart, "I do."

"David Eugene Porco, do you take this woman to be your lawfully wedded wife."

David opened his mouth to agree, but Jules held up her hand to stop him.

"Hold on a moment," she said. "Porco?"

"Yes?" David frowned at her.

"Your last name is Porco? I thought it was a nickname. Like, something cruel that kids called you that stuck."

"No, it's me. David Porco. But I like that you call me David."

Jules nodded her head slowly, as though she was trying to absorb this new detail and let it settle. "So, I'm going to be Julia...Porco?"

"Yes, Starflower. Is that okay with you?"

The grin that she'd found mischievous not too long ago caused Jules's features to pinch in annoyance. What was in a name? Beneath the twinge of indignation at this name-calling interlude, Jules's feelings hadn't changed for this man.

"Yes, it's okay," she croaked.

They both looked at Pastor Vance. The man held his tongue for a long moment. He didn't say the part asking if there was any reason this marriage shouldn't take place to speak now or forever hold their peace. He didn't need to say it. His silence spoke volumes.

When neither Jules nor David voiced any

opposition, he continued. "Then by the powers vested in me, I now pronounce you man and wife. You may kiss the bride."

David turned to her. He didn't hesitate. His hands were just as sure as they'd been back up in the Ferris wheel. His lips were just as certain as the first time they'd brushed hers. His sigh of utter contentment when he pulled away from her was just as satisfied as her own.

"Whatever may come," he whispered in her ear. "You're mine now."

"I am," she agreed. "And you're mine."

# CHAPTER FIFTEEN

The drive to the commune was quiet. Porco expected to feel differently now that he was married. But he didn't. He felt the same as he had after the first moment he saw Jules.

The same hum of energy skittered across the underside of his forearm, over the pulsing of the veins of his wrist to land in the palm of his hand. The same trickle of warmth pooled in the palm of his hand and radiated out to zing back up his arm and to his chest. The same sense of wholeness settled in his chest, easing the ache that had plagued his heart since he comprehended there was a thing in this world called love.

And now he had it.

While Porco turned the steering wheel with his

left hand, Jules's left hand rested in his right one. Her fingertips slid up from his palm and found their way to entwining with his. He folded his thick fingers down over her slender ones, locking the two of them into place.

He'd watched his parents fit together like two pieces of a puzzle for his whole life. His parents never made him feel like an outsider, but even as a kid, Porco was keenly aware that he was one half waiting for a whole. Now with Jules by his side, he felt a connection around the edges of him. The longer he spent with her, the closer he got to her, he felt the two of them snapping into place. He was certain that by morning, he would be made whole.

When he climbed out of the car, the night wind nipped at his back, brushing a cool tendril of air across his shoulders. He brushed it off as he rounded the truck to hand out his wife.

The feel of her hand in his reignited the spark. The cold from the twilight gushed out of him. Porco felt his center of gravity restoring itself.

"This is me," she said, pointing to a small cottage tucked away out in the back of the commune.

The structure was a one-story ranch made with a mix of brick and wood. There was a white bricked turret off to one side with an upside-down ice cream cone painted purple on the top. All it needed was a white flag billowing down and a princess leaning out the window.

"My father built it," Jules said, pride evident in her voice.

Porco wasn't surprised. It definitely looked man-made. It also looked like a strong gust of wind might blow it over. It didn't matter. If that's where Jules lived, then it was now his home too. He'd follow this woman anywhere, even if it was across the threshold of a children's storybook.

"Can you just wait here a second," she said. "I want to warn my sister first. She might've expected me to come home with a stuffed animal, but not a... you." She looked him up and down, eying his chest appreciatively.

Porco preened under her perusal. Under his wife's perusal. In just a matter of moments, he would unveil more of himself for her scrutiny. And he would gently, patiently coax her to do the same for him. For now, he waited on the threshold of her doorstep.

Jules slipped inside the door -the unlocked door. With a shy smile, she shut the flimsy piece of wood in front of his face. Again, he heard no snick of a lock. Looking at the brass handle, he saw no place for a keyhole.

So, not only did no one lock their doors on this land, but they didn't even have locks? That was insanity. It was a change that he would be making in the morning. He had no intention of ever leaving his wife unguarded when he wasn't present. Nor when he let down his guard as he slept with her in his arms.

Another chilling thought took him. If they didn't lock the front doors, then they had no cause to lock bedroom doors. What about bathroom doors? That would need to change. It might be that this would be the first argument they would have as a married couple. Not wanting anything to disrupt his honeymoon night, he would have to let the discussion hold until morning.

A tap at his shoulder brought Porco's attention around. He couldn't make out the figure standing behind him in the dark. He assumed it was a male by the broad shoulders. He became certain the person was male by the meaty fist that struck his eye and snapped his head back.

Porco doubled over, pressing the heel of his hand to his injured eye. Knowing that the threat was still near, he stepped back, putting his body between

Jules's door and the assailant. With his instincts kicking in, he straightened, ignoring the throbbing pain of his face. He balled his free hand in a fist and squared off against his opponent.

"Sneaking onto my land?" snarled his foe.

"This is my house." Well, it was his wife's house, and there was that fifty percent marital law. But Porco didn't bother explaining any of that. He had to first contend with neutralizing the menace.

"You must be sniffing those chemicals you poison the land with. If you won't go, I will remove you forcibly."

The man lunged for him. Porco easily outmaneuvered him with only one hand. It wasn't as easy as it looked. The guy was tall, mostly limbs. But there was a cord of power to him. Still, he was no match for a trained Army Ranger.

Porco took him down in two moves. The first move was a swipe with his boots that took out the man's legs. With his second move, Porco was on him. His fist was drawn back, ready to strike. But he stopped when he saw Jules coming towards him, a garden hoe raised for an attack. She wasn't looking at the intruder on the ground. Her gaze was focused on Porco.

"Jules," he said, ducking. "What are you doing?"

"What are you doing trying to break into my house," said Jules. Though her voice had gone an octave deeper. And when had she cut off her glorious locks? Her hair was short, a puffed-out cloud around her head.

"Romey, stop."

Porco was seeing double. Jules stood in the open doorway of her house. And Jules stood hovering over him with a weaponized gardening tool.

"Romey," said Jules in the doorway. "Put that down."

"He was trying to break into your house," said the man on the ground. Another look let Porco know it was the yogini laying on the ground.

“No, Paris,” said Jules coming to stand beside Porco. “I invited him in.”

"Why would you invite the enemy in?" asked Paris, now coming to a crouch.

"He's not the enemy," said Jules. "He's my husband."

The other Jules, Romey, let the gardening hoe clatter to the ground. In, Paris, rose to his full height. He took a menacing step towards Porco. Porco's head throbbed from the man's blow, but he was ready to take him on again.

Porco wouldn’t have to. Jules stepped in front of

him, as though she would protect him. Porco felt another click of their souls fitting into place.

"What's happened?" said Paris. "Has he tricked you? I know this one. Porco, isn't it? They call him that because he's a glutton for female attention."

Jules bristled, but she didn't move away from Porco. "No, that's his last name. Now it's my name, too."

Both Romey and Paris stared, mouths agape as though they were the fish out of water on their own land. Romey was the first to shake off the shock.

"I thought you were just going on a date," said Jules's twin. "How did this happen?"

"It's him," Jules said. "He's The One. There's a spark between us."

Romey's face didn't light up as Jules's was now doing. Romey pinched the bridge of her nose and looked to the stars as if they would provide her any answers.

"You got married?" said Paris.

Jules turned to the man. Was that a touch of guilt on her face? "Yes, I got married."

"But he's a soldier. He's a carnivore. That belt he's wearing is made of leather."

They all looked down at Porco's belt. Paris was right. The belt was leather. So, what of it?

When Paris's gaze lifted from Porco's belt, he looked ready to skin him alive. Not willing to turn the other cheek, Porco took a fighting stance. But Romey stepped between the two men.

"Paris, it looks like you need a visit to the Problem Jar."

Whatever the Problem Jar was, it didn't look as though it sounded inviting to Paris. The man glared at Romey, then Porco, then Jules.

"Paris, I'm sorry," said Jules. "You've been a really good friend to me over the years. But I never felt more for you than deep friendship. I should've told you that sooner."

Under the pale moonlight, Paris's cheeks puffed red in anger. He took a step back from Jules, as though the force of the emotion was unexpected. He turned the full force of that glare on Porco. "You're not welcome here. You will never be welcome here."

Paris turned and walked away. As he made his way up the path, a huge pig made its way down the path. The animal gave the man a wide berth. Its attention caught on Porco, and it trotted over to him.

Porco hadn't seen many live pigs in his life. His father's people were from the country, and when they'd gone to visit, he'd seen hogs roasted over the fire. Which was why he'd learned never to play with his favorite food.

But this pig had decided they would be friends. It nuzzled its snout against Porco's jeans. Insistent until Porco gave his hairy head a pat.

"Well, at least Hamlet likes you," said Romey.

Porco looked up at Jules's sister, her twin. He saw the differences clearly now. Romey had frown lines marring her brow. There wasn't the same light twinkling in her hazel depths. Her arms were crossed over her chest, and her features cast a shade of skepticism in his direction. He'd have to win her over, but he hadn't the first clue how.

"Jules, what is going on?" said her twin. "Tell me you didn't marry a man you just met this morning."

"Okay, I won't tell you that. Even though it's a fact."

Romey sighed.

"Hi, I'm Porco, your new brother." When Romey grimaced at his last name, Porco amended, "You can call me David, like your sister does."

Still no response from his new sister-in-law. She only gaped at him as though she couldn't believe he was real.

"Come on inside," said Jules. "Let's get that eye looked at."

The three of them walked into the house, followed by the pig. Porco was about to voice an objection, his family hadn't even allowed dogs in the house. However, once inside, Porco saw a nest of cushions with the word Hamlet painted over top. Apparently, the pig was not only not food, it was some kind of a pet.

With Jules's hands on his face, he forgot about the pig in the corner of the room. The throb behind his eye eased a bit, but he was sure he'd have a shiner in the morning. He just couldn't believe he'd let that wispy farmer yogini get the drop on him. It had been more than the element of surprise, Porco was off his game because his head was in the clouds because of the woman peering intently into his wounded eye.

"It'll be fine," he assured Jules. "You got any raw meat in the fridge to bring the swelling down?"

Jules's head waggled in that comical way when another person says something utterly ridiculous. But what had he said that was nonsense?

"Paris is right," said Romey. "He won't be accepted here."

# CHAPTER SIXTEEN

David was quiet as they drove the short distance from the commune to the ranch next door. Jules had never been on the property. She'd driven past it plenty of times over the years. The main difference was the number of cows that dotted the green pastures where crops and colorful dwellings dotted her homeland.

The light of the moon shone the way as they drove up to the big house. There weren't near as many houses on this ranch as there were on the commune. Far fewer people as well. She felt a stab of disappointment that David hadn't gotten to visit the nightly bonfire on the commune. But Paris's words hung in her mind. Would anyone ever accept him on the land?

She'd always thought of the people of her home as the most open-minded, the most compassionate, the most accepting of differences. And they were. Except when it came to the Vances and how they treated the land.

David wasn't a farmer. He wasn't even a rancher. He was a friend, helping out another friend. He didn't even understand the meaning of the word organic, or vegan for that matter. Was he willing to learn? When he did, would he take her side? Was the thought of making him take aside a problematic way of thinking?

Jules let out a long sigh. Before she'd extinguished all the air in her lungs, she felt warmth kindling in the palm of her hands. David had reached for her hand. He'd engulfed her fingers with his own. At that moment, Jules knew there were no sides. There were only the two of them, standing together, back to back, face to face or side by side to take on whatever may come at them.

Jules looked over at the man who she had changed her entire world for. She wasn't sure what the future held for them, but she knew that being by his side was the right decision. She would give her family and friends time. They would come around. They had to.

At the end of the long drive, David put the car in park. He turned to her with a wary smile. He looked as tired as she felt. The wound beneath his eye was turning a darker shade.

"You alright?" he asked.

"I'm fine," she said, proud her voice held no sign of trembling, unlike her fingers. "We should get that looked at."

She lifted her hand to his face. David caught her fingers before she could touch his eye. He pressed a kiss to each of her five digits.

"Brenda will have some raw meat in the fridge. That and some ice is all it will take."

"I don't understand what you want meat for. Or ice for that matter? You need a warm compress with arnica."

"That sounds like poison," he grinned, brushing her fingertips over his bottom lip.

"Only if you ingest it." Jules watched her fingertips as they glided across his mouth. She wanted to take her hands away and replace them with her mouth.

"Is this our first argument?" David asked, nipping at her index finger. "How to handle the wound your boyfriend just gave me?"

"Paris was never my boyfriend. He wanted more.

I didn't. I should've said something a long time ago, but I didn't want to hurt his feelings."

"I'm just messing with you." David pressed her hand to his heart. It leaped the moment her fingers touched his chest. "I don't blame Frenchie."

"His name is Paris." Jules grinned up at David, getting instantly lost in those dark eyes. What were they talking about?

"I'd knock out any guy who tried to come between you and me." David brushed a kiss against her forehead. Then over her eyelid. Then on each cheek. "If he comes at me again, I will knock him across the country."

Jules pulled away from her husband. She set her mouth to tell him that she did not condone violence. But the strength in his tone did something to her belly. It called her a liar.

She was certain she didn't want to see Paris hurting any more than he was. But she liked the idea of David using his strong body to protect her. She was moments away from being fully introduced to her husband's body. They just needed to get out of this truck and to his room. Oh, and there was that matter with his bruise that needed tending to first.

David let go of her hand to climb out of his truck. She watched as he made his way around to her, enjoying the way his long legs ate up the ground to get to her. When he reached her in just a few strides, Jules voiced something that had niggled her on the drive over.

"Paris said you were a glutton for female attention," she said when David had opened the door for her.

David reached into the cab of the truck. He put his hands on her hips and lifted her out as though she weighed nothing. "I told you I'd dated a lot."

"And now you're done with that." Jules wrapped her arms around his neck as he pulled her against him, holding her just off the ground.

"Yes." He held her so that her head was just a hair higher than his. He gazed up at her as though she was the sun and moon and stars combined.

It took Jules a moment to find her voice. "Why me?"

"You know why?" He held her against him with one hand. With the other, he brushed a stray lock back behind her ear. "You feel it too."

She nodded. The spark had grown into a fire between them. With each moment they spent close to one another, it blazed ever brighter. She started to wonder if it would burn them someday.

"Come on," he said, carefully setting her feet on the ground. "Let's get you inside."

They walked hand in hand. They were nearer to the side of the house, so they rounded to the back. As they approached, Jules heard voices. She smelled something sweet in the air. It was an unfamiliar scent mixed with the familiar smell of burning wood and charcoal.

So, the Vance Ranch had bonfires of their own. That settled her anxiety. There would be some familiarity with this bunch.

And then she saw it.

People were gathered around a fire, much like the nightly bonfires on the commune. But unlike the bonfires where people sat with musical instruments on their laps, and others danced around the blaze, there was something in this fire.

Speared on a stake was the carcass of a pig. Its sightless eyes stared at her accusingly. Men poked at it with a stick and sharp knives.

“Hey, Porco, we made your favorite.”

Porco raised his free hand and waved. Jules placed her free hand over her mouth to stifle the guttural scream that ached to rise. All laughter around the bonfire faded when they saw her.

“What’s she doing here?”

Jules had never met Brenda Vance in person, but she'd seen the woman many times. Brenda rose from her seat and advanced on the two of them. The female rancher looked anything but welcoming.

The fight had gone out of Jules. She was feeling far too queasy watching the animal turning and burning on the fire. "I need to lie down," she said to David.

# CHAPTER SEVENTEEN

There was a pain in his neck when he woke the next morning. His eye throbbed a bit as well. But all that pain went away when Porco inhaled.

The flowery scent of lavender tickled the fine hairs of his nose. Followed by the burning bite of peppermint. That overwhelming scent was chased down with a breeze of vanilla, so sweet that he opened his mouth to sample a lick. Instead of an ice cream cone, Porco's lips met with a lush field of silky brown.

Jules lay beside him in his bed, still deep in sleep. They both rested on top of the sheets, covered in their clothing they'd worn on their date. The same clothing they'd worn at their wedding. It wasn't the wedding night he'd always dreamed of, being that he sported a black eye from when he'd tried to carry her over her home's threshold, and she'd thrown up after bearing witness to the reception she'd gotten when they'd arrived at his home.

Porco and Jules's relationship had been rushed, out of order, and out of whack. Gazing down at his wife, he knew that he'd take every step again if it led him to this moment with her in his arms. The disaster of the other day hadn't dampened the spark he felt for this woman. Still, he had no idea what step to take next in their lives.

When they'd come inside the bungalow to his room, she had collapsed on the bed. He'd sat down beside her with a cold compress to his eye since all the meat in the house was cooking in the fire. Besides, she'd had such a bad reaction to the pig roasting that he didn't want to upset her even more.

Before he'd closed his good eye, he'd done a quick google search on the word vegan. His stomach growled even now, remembering its definition. Not only did his wife not eat any meat, she also didn't eat any dairy. He didn't understand how she lived. Certainly not how she had the curves that she did.

Would she expect him to give up meat as well? He was still trying to resign himself to the idea that she wouldn't be making him a plate of bacon and eggs this morning. But one more whiff of her hair and Porco was ready to forgo bacon... for breakfast at least.

He had no idea what to offer her to break her fast? Maybe some home fried potatoes? A salad? If he could find any greens. The only salad he knew how to make was potato salad. And he always put heavy cream in it. So that was a no go.

He knew what vegans didn't eat. But he had no clue as to what they did.

With great reluctance, Porco disentangled himself from his sleeping wife. It was a hardship. Moving away from her felt like tearing himself from a bound book. The pages of their lives may not have started off in the same place. But after being glued together, the story of their lives wouldn't make sense if the pages went missing.

He found the strength to step away from her. He made his way into the bathroom that he shared with Spinelli and Rusty. It looked as though the other two men had already risen and made their way out into the fields. Looking into the bathroom mirror, Porco caught the shiner below his eye. It wasn't as bad as it felt. It was more of his Army Pride that had taken a hit. He'd been cold-cocked by a vegan. How had Paris gotten so big if the male didn't eat meat?

Porco showered and dressed. Keaton had told him to take the day off, but he was used to getting up at the crack of dawn and getting his hands dirty. Outside, the day was overcast. Rain threatened, but he could see the sun peeking out behind the clouds. It could go either way.

"We weren't expecting you," said Rusty. The man wore army fatigues and cowboy boots. It was how most of the soldiers on the two neighboring ranches dressed; a mirroring of their old and new lives. "You and the missus already fighting?"

"No, she's still asleep. We had a long day."

"I'll say," said Rusty. "What with meeting and then getting married right after, it was busy."

"Not you too," Porco sighed.

Rusty had been the only man in their unit that had been married. Though that was soon coming to an end. Not because Rusty wanted his marriage to end. Porco had watched the man fight for his marriage for the last year, offering Veronica anything she wanted. The demand Ronni came back with? She wanted nothing more from him except his signature on the divorce papers. Each morning Rusty struggled, pen in hand, to give her that. Of all of his friends, Porco had thought that Rusty would champion his marriage. Apparently, he was wrong.

"Did you even think it through?" asked Rusty. "Divorces aren't a walk in the park."

"We're not getting a divorce."

Rusty lifted his eyebrows as if to say, *That might be what you think*. His gaze looked up at the clouds. They'd darkened to gray.

Porco's gaze searched the sky too. He knew that behind those clouds the sun would break out at any moment. He just had to wait for it.

"Even if she wanted a divorce," which Porco hoped with everything in him that Jules didn't want, "it wouldn't mean anything. I gave her more than my vow last night, I gave her my heart. It's hers forever. Whether she wants it or not."

"Yeah," said Rusty. "I know exactly what you mean."

## CHAPTER EIGHTEEN

Jules woke up alone in bed. Which would not be out of the ordinary. Except she had woken a few times in the night and felt the warm, sure heat of David behind her.

Though the previous day had been trying, she'd remembered her reasons for being here with this man in the night. David had held her tightly to him as she'd slept. All through the night, in a strange bed, on land she wasn't sure she was welcome on, she'd felt as though she were fitting into him like a puzzle piece. At the sharp pointed edges of David's body where he ended, she'd begun to curve into him forging a new beginning.

Jules had always felt that something had been

missing in her life. Now she knew that something had been a someone. That someone had been him.

So, where was he?

All around the room, she saw evidence of him. A green army-issued duffle bag sat at the floor of the open closet. Inside the closet, jeans and fatigues were organized from the darkest shades to the lightest on hangers. Shirts hung crisp, not only going from light to dark, but also organized by collared shirts, t-shirts, and flannel.

So, her husband was a neat freak. That was good. Though Jules's closet back home was nowhere near this organized and color-coded, everything was at least on hangers and in drawers.

*At home.* The words echoed into her ears. Was this her new home? Was there space for her here? And what about Hamlet? He was technically her pet. Romey just tolerated his presence. No way was Jules bringing the pig anywhere near this ranch. Her stomach roiled to think back to what she'd seen last night.

Jules rose from the bed. She was still in the clothes she'd worn the other day. In her haste to leave the commune last night, she'd forgotten to pack any of her clothes with her. Her sundress was wrinkled and rumpled. She must look a fright. She was glad at that moment that David wasn't there to see her.

A knock sounded at her door. It seemed entirely wrong that her husband should knock on their bedroom door before entering. If things had gone as planned last night, her wedding night, then David would've probably still been in bed with her. And her clothes wouldn't have been wrinkled from sleep. They'd have been in a heap on the floor.

Jules padded barefoot over to answer the door. On the other side wasn't the man she was expecting. There wasn't a man standing there at all.

"Good morning, I'm Patty." The redhead wore a bright and friendly smile.

"Hi," said Jules. Jules had a vague memory of seeing the woman around the bonfire the other night. When her gaze had slid away from the fire, it had landed on something else red. Yes, she remembered that red hair. "I'm Jules."

"Well, I know that, silly. I'm your official welcome wagon." Patty held a plate in her hands. "Porco said you were vegan. That means no meat, right? Which is a challenge for me because it's all I know how to cook. Luckily, I know how to scramble an egg."

"Well, eggs are meat."

Patty's smile faltered. She looked down at the

plate of fluffy, yellow eggs and frowned. Her gaze took in the eggs anew as though she were seeing them for the first time.

"They are?" Patty's voice rang with bewilderment. Then her features crumpled in embarrassment. She slapped a hand at her forehead. "Right, I guess the egg came before the chicken."

She let out a self-deprecating laugh. Jules joined her, not wanting to turn away the first friendly face on this ranch.

"There's also fruit and bagels," said Patty. "Are those okay?"

"Those are fine," Jules lied, taking the plate. Though fruits and bagels were a staple of her diet, the fruit and bagel on the plate were not only touching the eggs, they also sat in a vat of eggy butter.

"Thank you," Jules said. She thought she might content herself with the top of the bagel. But alas, there was cream cheese on the bagel. Still, it was the thought that counted.

"I also brought you some clothes since I didn't see you come in with any bags or anything."

Patty handed over a colorful sundress. Though Patty's offering cost more than Jules's annual clothing budget. Beggars couldn't be choosers. Jules was again grateful.

"The boys are out at the camp this morning," said Patty. "I'm going to get lunch started if you want to come up to the big house. I'm making catfish. You can have fish, right?"

"Nope." Jules gave a shake of her head. "Fish is meat. So..."

"Hmmm." But then Patty brushed it off. "We'll figure something out. Welcome to the family."

## CHAPTER NINETEEN

"Yogurt, that's gotta be vegan. Right?" Porco held up the packaged containers. The bright label announced healthy alerts like sugar-free, fat-free, real fruit, and something to do with active cultures.

"No, that has dairy. Dairy is from cows." Spinelli spoke in slow clipped tones as though he were talking to a child.

Porco scowled at his friend. He hadn't asked the man to come along on his grocery store run. Spinelli had hopped into the passenger seat as Porco had started up the truck. At first, Porco hadn't minded the company. Spinelli was a high intellect guy and could help him navigate the labyrinth that was veganism. Porco would've made many more mistakes if his high intellect friend hadn't come along on the errand. Porco just wished Spinelli had a bit more emotional intelligence at the moment.

"If it has a face, it's not a vegetable," Spinelli said for the tenth time.

How was Porco to know what had had a face if it wasn't bleeding in the package? Already he'd had to take out butter from his cart. He'd never realized it came from cows. A packet of tuna had been nixed - because the chicken of the sea was, well, meat. Even a can of brown beans had been blocked because, when they'd turned the can around and read the label, Spinelli pointed out that it was made with bacon seasonings.

Once again, the cruel truth seized him; David Porco had married a woman who'd never tasted and would never want a slice of warm, crispy, salty-sweet bacon. She had a pet pig, for goodness sake. Porco couldn't even think about Hamlet without his stomach grumbling.

"I have no idea what to feed my wife."

It was Porco's job to provide for and protect Jules. Already he was doing a poor job at that. She was even now in his bedroom, which wasn't even his own home, with nothing to wear, which on any other day wouldn't be a problem, and nothing to eat. A fine husband he was turning out to be.

He wanted to give Jules the world. He just didn't know which parts would suit her? A hand came down on his shoulder, giving him an awkward *there-there* pat.

"Just stick to the fruits and vegetables on the outer perimeter, and you'll be fine."

Porco glanced up at his friend. It was a rare show of humanity from the cyborg in the group. Usually, Spinelli was all facts and numbers. Emotions simply didn't compute in his oversized brain.

Just as quickly as Spinelli had offered the fleeting comfort, did he snatch his hand back, clenching and releasing his fists with the same awkwardness. "I mean, even a trained monkey couldn't screw that up."

And the moment was gone.

"She makes my heart speed up, man. She puts butterflies in my stomach."

"That's not love," said Spinelli. "That's a medical condition."

Porco sighed, knowing he'd never get The Cyborg to understand what he was feeling. Spinelli wasn't even listening to Porco any longer. His gaze was fixed on something on the other side of the store.

Still, Porco was thankful for the friend at his side. Thankful that Spinelli was trying to help him care for Jules in the only way his genius friend knew how. Before he'd left the ranch, he'd passed Patty who was at work making Jules breakfast. On his way to his truck, Keaton had insisted that Porco take the next couple of days off. Brenda, who'd stood at her husband's side, had chewed at her lip but remained mute. That was the best Porco could hope from the strong woman; silence instead of a tongue lashing.

He knew his friends would put aside the conflict between the ranches and accept Jules. Especially once they got to know her. Once they looked into her eyes, they'd see she was nothing but kindness. Once they listened to her speak, they'd witness her wit and want to talk with her for hours. Once they heard her laugh, they'd know they'd found a true friend. She would capture their hearts as she had done with his.

"Hey, Porco."

Porco looked up to find a leggy brunette eyeing him like he was on one of the fruit platters he was considering for his wife. He gave the woman a polite nod and turned back to the produce. On a low shelf, he saw a package labeled tofu. The item sounded familiar, though he'd knew he'd never had it before.

"I'm excited about tonight."

Porco glanced up. The brunette was still there. In fact, she was closer to him, all up in his personal space like she had a right to be there. She lifted a hand to him, her finger poised to run over his chest.

There was a sizzle in the air, hovering in the inch between her finger and his exposed skin. It crackled in his ear like electricity. It hummed like the purr of an engine ready to take off.

Porco watched the woman's finger, partly in fascination but mostly in horror. How could there be a spark between them after he'd found Jules? Had he been wrong about her?

Even before the thought fully formed in his head, he'd dismissed it. What was happening between him and this woman was a sizzle, a crackle. Jules had been an explosion.

Jules had made his heart stop.

Jules had invaded his mind.

Jules had felt like she was part of his soul.

When the woman's finger landed on his chest, Porco eyed it curiously. His heart didn't skip a beat. His brain was foggy with thoughts of Jules. His soul was restless, eager to get back to his wife.

His mind wanted her so much that he thought he was seeing things. Standing at the front of the store, Porco saw Spinelli wincing in his direction. Beside his friend, stood his wife.

But it was odd. Every time Porco was in the same space as Jules, his heart sped up. His mouth would water. The palms of his hands would itch. None of that happened now.

Perhaps it was because Jules's hazel eyes sparked in anger. Her pouty lips pinched in disgust. She turned on her heel and marched out the door. Her short, curly hair bouncing in the retreat.

Short curly hair? Not Jules. Uh oh.

"Porco?" said the brunette, leaning into him.

Porco had forgotten she was even there. He tore his gaze from Romey's retreating form. He had no idea what Spinelli had said to Jules's twin to tick her off. Probably something to do with the idiotic feud between the two ranches. Instead of staying, Spinelli hurried out the door after Romey.

"I can't wait to see you tonight," said the brunette.

"Tonight?"

"Yeah, for the concert." Her sultry grin faltered. "Remember?"

"Oh!" Porco's Jules-haze cleared from his brain momentarily. "It's Paige, right?"

"Right," she said, taking a step back from him.

"We had a date tonight. Sorry, I can't."

"Don't tell me you're back with Rosalind."

"Rosalind? No, she dumped me a few days ago. I got married last night."

"Married? You?"

"I actually need to get back to my wife now. She's probably starving. Do you know how to cook tofu?"

## CHAPTER TWENTY

What had she done?

After her full breakfast of air pie and wind pudding, Jules decided she needed a second helping of fresh air. She pulled on clothes that weren't her own and left out of the front door of a house that wreaked of man, to walk across foreign soil that felt so distant from her homeland.

In reality, it was only a thirty-minute walk through the fields of Vance Ranch to reach the boundary line that separated it from the Verona Commune. The green pastures of the cattle ranch turned from green to brown the further she moved from east to west. Only to turn green again, the closer she came to her home.

The small cabin she shared with her sister was

settled at the edge of the property. Her mother had chosen that part of the land because the soil was dryer there, not as rich as the land further toward the center of the commune. It was land where beans could thrive.

From this distance, Jules could spy some of her soy beanstalks. She'd taken care not to plant too close to the boundary, not wanting any of her crops to encroach on the Vance Ranch. Still, it looked like the beans had a mind of their own.

On a strip a few yards closest to the border, a patch of seedlings had pushed their way through the dry earth. They shouldn't have been strong enough to have driven through such packed and infertile ground. But push they did through the barren land. Still, it was strange that it was just this small patch of earth that showed life and not further along the boundary.

Jules's mind turned from the tenacious beans to her homeland. She couldn't see the communal fire pit that brought her community together each night, but she thought she could scent the cinders on the wind. She couldn't see the creek she'd swum in naked and unashamed when she was a child but thought she felt its damp waters settle on her brow. She couldn't see the home she'd lived in her entire life, but she felt a connection to it across the short distance.

Did she want to go back home? Did she want to leave this strange land? Did she want to move past these people who were so different than the ones she'd grown up with?

David's grin popped into her mind, clouding her vision. Instead of the light breeze from across the way, she felt the press of his thumb on her cheek. Instead of the dampness of the creek water, she remembered the heat that came when he pressed his lips to hers. Instead of the creaky floorboards of her family's little cabin, she heard the deep rumble of his laughter in her ears.

That's when she knew it. Home was now, and would forever be, wherever he was.

Jules wrapped her arms around herself. Even though she was by herself in a field of barren earth, she knew she wasn't alone. Her husband was out in the world. She sensed that, wherever he was, he was thinking of her at this moment.

The sound of hooves impacting the ground brought her back to the present. Jules's heart sped up, wondering if it was David riding up to swoop her onto a horse and ride off with her. Her heart slowed its beating in disappointment to see that the rider atop the horse sported a ponytail.

Brenda Vance.

Unlike the smile Patty had given her, Brenda Vance scowled when she saw Jules. "I can't figure you out."

Brenda dismounted, still keeping the reins of the horse wound in one hand. Her pretty features were pensive, but her other hand was gentle on the horse's mane. Never one to leave an animal unpetted, Jules stepped closer to the horse and ran her hand over its long nose.

Brenda raised her hand, as though to caution Jules. But the animal dipped its head for Jules's touch.

"He's not the most friendly beast," said Brenda.

Jules shrugged as she ran her hand over the horse's ears. It neighed in delight. "Never met an animal that didn't mind a little affection; be he man or beast."

"Is this where you tell me to spare the lives of my cattle?"

Jules huffed, her laugh humorless. "Even though I was homeschooled, my daddy taught us Darwinism. I know humans are omnivores; what with the molars and the canines in our mouths. I just choose not to eat meat. I don't judge others who are different than me."

"Well then, you're a rarity in these parts." Brenda turned away from Jules, angling her body so that it was perpendicular to the horse. "I'm judged every day because I'm a cattle rancher with the wrong body parts. Though if I had those other parts, I know mine would be bigger than the male ranchers around here."

Jules giggled at that. Sexism was less of a problem in a community that prized equality, but it still reared its head at times. Like when everyone expected her to marry Paris without a thought of what she wanted to do with her life, her heart.

"What?" said Brenda. "Like you've had to deal with sexism over on your hippie farm of equality?"

"Paris wanted me to marry him. When I married David instead, he kicked me off the land."

"Well, it that isn't the definition of fascism and patriarchy, I don't know what is?"

Jules inhaled deeply and let out a weary sigh. "No. That's not him. Paris is a good man. He's just very focused on securing the future of our land."

Listen to her. Jules was still saying *our land* even though she was standing on the wrong side of the boundary.

"I don't think he ever considered marrying someone that didn't live on the land," Jules continued. "Since we always got along so well, I think he figured I was the best candidate."

"Sounds... sterile."

Jules tilted her head to look up at the tall brunette. "Isn't that the marriage you'd planned for you and your husband."

Brenda opened her mouth to argue. Before any words came out, she winced, as though she thought better of what she planned to say. When she looked at Jules once more, her stern features appeared sheepish.

"You and I," said Jules, "we're probably more alike than you think."

"Maybe," conceded Brenda. Then she wrinkled her nose. "Except for our diet. Where do you get your protein?"

"Same place the cows do; the grass."

Brenda blinked as though she'd never made the connection. Most people forgot that cows were vegans.

"Soybean is high in protein," Jules continued, putting on her farmer's hat. "Studies show it's a great substitute crop for cattle. Especially if you want certified organic beef, which is all the rage these days."

Like the horse, Brenda's ears perked up. But she said nothing. The two women stood there in companionable silence for a moment. In the space between them, it was as though a rift was healing. Fertile ground filling the cracks left by generations before them.

"So, you… and Porco?" Brenda turned her head back to Jules, studying her eyes just like her pastor brother. Though Brenda's eyes had a steeliness to them where Pastor Vance was all softness. "How is that even going to work?"

A grin spread across Jules's face at the thought of her husband. The hunger that was present in her belly had less to do with food and more to do with a desire for him. Jules and David might have a different diet, but one thing she knew for sure was that her appetite would only ever be satisfied by him.

## CHAPTER TWENTY-ONE

Porco grabbed the brown grocery bags from the passenger seat and kicked the door shut with his booted heel. Spinelli had stayed behind in town, waving Porco off as he trailed after Jules's sister. Had there been interest in the typically discerning man's eyes? Wouldn't that be something if his best friend and his wife's sister ended up together?

The grocery bag wobbled in Porco's arms as he tried to juggle the keys in one hand and his cell phone in the other. He realized belatedly that he didn't have his wife's cell phone number. He didn't remember her bringing one with her as they'd left her house the other day. Then he remembered her telling him that she didn't have one.

It wasn't quite afternoon, just late morning. Porco figured Jules would be up by now. Would she have ventured around the ranch? He tried to imagine the place from her eyes.

Angel, the sole ranch hand that had actually been hired to work the land and animals, was eying one herd of cattle with tags dangling from their ears. The young man's dark eyes were discerning as his pencil scratched on a notepad in hand, writing down the numbers. Porco knew he was determining which cattle were headed for slaughter.

He didn't want Jules to see that. Not after the roasting pig last night. They couldn't stay here on the ranch. But neither could they live on the commune.

The first order of business today would be to find a place in town where they could live. Or maybe even a starter ranch with land for her to grow her beloved beans. He wasn't a big spender, and he had plenty saved up to make the purchase. Not to mention that the investment in the training camp was already paying off.

Porco would be able to provide for his wife and the family they would have one day. Just the thought of having a family with Jules made his stomach growl with want. Or maybe that was hunger. He needed to get inside and feed them both.

He found her in the small kitchen of the bungalow he shared with Spinelli and Rusty. She was crouched down at the open door of the fridge. Her beautiful features were screwed up in disappointment.

Porco's heart thumped. Not out of desire. The organ gave a sharp kick to his chest. If his heart had a voice, it would be calling him an idiot for failing to provide for his wife.

The inside of the fridge was mostly bare. Aside from a few cases of beer, energy drinks, and packages and packages of bacon.

"Hey," he said.

She glanced over her shoulder, her face lighting when she saw him. "Hey."

Porco's heart stopped its kicking and settled down in a flutter. The blood that had been rushing through his ears sighed now that he had a full view of her face. Julia Porco was the most beautiful sight he'd ever seen in his life. And she was all his.

"You came back," she said.

Every molecule, muscle, and tendon in Porco went slack. The grin that had started to rise went lax.

His knees threatened to buckle. His arms went slack, and he nearly lost the contents of the grocery bag.

"You thought I'd left you?" he asked.

They stared at each other for a moment. She sat back on her heels. He stood over her. Finally, Porco sat the groceries on the table and reached for her. Jules came willingly into his arms. She wrapped herself tightly around him, and Porco squeezed her even closer.

He'd been up for hours, but now he felt wide awake. He buried his nose in her thick locks. The scents of vanilla and lavender signaling that no matter where on this earth he stood, he was exactly where he was supposed to be.

"I don't know what I thought?" Jules mumbled into his neck. "David, I don't know how this is going to work?"

Porco pulled back but did not let her go. He cupped her chin in his hand as he gazed into those hypnotic hazel eyes. "Do you want it to work?"

Without a second's hesitation, Jules nodded. The golden flecks in her eyes burned bright. "This all just happened so fast."

He pressed a kiss between her brows. Her eyelids fluttered against his chin. Her soft exhale warmed his neck. He knew then that if her answer had been in the negative, it would not have deterred him. He would've followed this woman to the ends of the earth. Even if that meant a few miles down the road to the lands he was not welcome on.

"David, we are so different. And we don't even know each other, not really."

"What do you want to know? I'll tell you anything. I'll tell you everything."

"Well, you know I don't even have your phone number."

"I'll give it to you now." Still holding her to him with one arm, he pulled out his phone with the other. Then he paused. "I suppose I should get you a cell phone first?"

She grinned down at the device, then bit her lip as she looked back up at him. He was so focused on the place where her tooth had taken her lip. He wanted to do that. Then he realized he could.

Phone forgotten, Porco pressed his lips to hers. Jules gasped at the surprise contact. When her lips parted, Porco took advantage.

He deepened the kiss. He tightened his hold. He pressed his claim.

With his kiss, he wanted to impart his entire being to this woman. He needed her to know that he hid nothing from her. He needed her to know that he would give anything to her, do anything for her. When Porco broke the kiss, finally letting them both up for air, there was one thing he needed to know above all.

"Do you want to go back to the commune?”

Though she was clearly dazed from his kisses, Jules shook her head. “I want to be wherever you are."

Porco rested his cheek atop her head, finding a cushion in the soft coils he found there. "I didn't leave you. I went to get you something to eat."

With great reluctance, he let her go and reached for the grocery bag. Digging into his bounty of produce, he produced one packaged product.

"Tofu?" she said. "You got me tofu?"

“It’s soybeans? Right? It's what you grow, so I figured you would eat it."

"Yes," she grinned. "This is what I eat, and I’m starving. Come on, I'll make us lunch."

# CHAPTER TWENTY-TWO

"You hate it, don't you?"

Jules watched as David's mouth worked. His right cheek puffed out as he chewed the tofu she'd fried up for him with oil and the available spices. Lips pursing, David's right cheek hollowed as he shifted the bite of food to the left side of his mouth and continued to chew.

"It's not bad," he said, his throat working as he tried to swallow. He tried to lift the corners of his mouth into a grin, but he grimaced instead. He coughed, pounding on his chest. The bite stayed down. David lifted his head, grin firmly in place with his triumph.

"If you liked it," she said, not bothering to hide

the suspicion in her tone, "then why not have another bite."

Jules forked a bite of the spongy dish onto her own fork. She raised it to her husband's mouth, airplane style. David's grin of triumph faltered in defeat.

"It's fine," Jules laughed. "It's an acquired taste." She zoomed the fork for a landing in her own mouth.

David's gaze was rapt to her mouth as she chewed. The moment she swallowed, he dipped down to land his lips on hers for a kiss. "I think it's growing on me."

He pressed a kiss to her forehead and then rose from the chair. Tugging open the fridge door, he pulled out a package of bacon. Jules watched in silent dismay as her husband wrapped a strip of breakfast meat around the tofu she'd cooked, and then place it into the frying pan.

"I want you to be comfortable, Jules." Using a spatula, David flipped the sizzling meat wrapped tofu over to the other side.

Jules shifted in the hardback dining room chair. Her nose twitched as the salty-sweet smell of pork permeated the kitchen. "I'm comfortable."

David dished his concoction out of the pan and

onto a plate, returning to sit beside her. "I know no one else believes in what we have. But this is real for me."

Jules's gaze was locked on the illogical pairing her husband forked and lifted to his lips. "It's real for me too."

David chewed. His brows knitting together as the food hit his palate. And then, a smile of delight. "It's not bad. I could get used to this."

A drizzle of bacon grease slipped down the corners of his mouth. Jules reached out to him, using her thumb to wipe it away. Repulsion from the pork was the last thing on her mind.

"I love you," she said.

David's grin spread impossibly wider. His eyes lit up. Jules felt the sparks fly from his gaze to hers and settle in her heart. She didn't need him to say the words back. The very look on his face told her his feelings were the same.

She pressed her lips to his. And grimaced. Just as he found tofu to be an acquired taste, she was not jumping on the bacon bandwagon. It didn't matter. She'd trudge through an acre of slop to get closer to this man.

Jules pulled back, gazing into his eyes. She could sit and stare into them forever without an ounce of self-consciousness. Something outside the window tugged at her attention.

"Jules, I love-"

"Is that my sister?"

Jules rose from David's embrace to make her way to the side door of the bungalow. Sure enough, Romey leaned against their truck, speaking to a man. Jules recognized David's friend, Spinelli. The two of them were deep in conversation. Like Jules's gaze had been rapt on David a second ago, Romey appeared unable to take her eyes off the soldier before her.

In fact, her methodical-minded twin was leaning into Spinelli. And—no.

Did Romey just glance down and tuck her hair behind her ear in the universal girl language meaning *I'm interested*? Jules blinked twice, unable to believe her sister was looking up at a man under hooded lashes. Spinelli's full attention was fixed on Romey's face, intent on her every word and motion.

"I tried to tell my sister the same thing," Romey was saying. "This idea of romantic love is nothing but biology."

"Tell me about it." Spinelli tugged at his bottom lip. "Humans were designed to procreate, that's the push we all feel."

"Hmm," Romey agreed, twirling a lock with her index finger. "Though I do think its safest when procreation is done in a committed pair bond. Like wolves, or penguins."

"And owls. Did you know the male courts the female by bringing her dead mice."

"Fascinating," Romey sighed. "So, marriage does make sense in some cases. With the right person."

Spinelli took a step closer. "How would you qualify the right person?"

Now Romey tugged at her lower lip. Her gaze dipped to Spinelli's chest, where his muscles strained under the cotton of his t-shirt. "In most of the world, pairings are still largely transactional. People wed for land, for money, for power."

"I suppose that makes sense," Spinelli agreed. "Though compatibility should probably come into factor at some point. Say, if two people both had the same logical mindset, found interests in the same topics like science... that might make sense."

Romey tilted her head back. "Yes, I suppose it might."

Jules couldn't take the awkward, intellectual flirting any longer. "Hello."

Romey and Spinelli broke apart. Guilt colored each of their cheeks. Behind her, Jules heard David chuckling softly. He might have whispered, “Finally.” But she had no idea what he could mean by that.

Romey’s guilty gaze shifted from her sister to her husband. Her shoulders straightened, and her finger lifted to point at David. "I just came from the grocery store where I saw him with another woman.”

“Well, he wasn’t *with* Paige.” Spinelli spread his hands in placation. “She came up to him.”

Romey turned back to Spinelli. “She was clearly flirting with him.”

“You’re right. She was.” Spinelli turned to David. “But was he flirting with her?”

Romey turned to David. Jules tilted her head, waiting for her husband’s answers. He had eyes for no one but her.

“Paige and I had a date for tonight,” David said.

Jules heard the sound of ticking. A bomb was set to go off in her chest. David opened his mouth to say more, but she wasn’t sure she could handle a second trigger.

“I let her know that I wasn’t going to make it on account of I’m married now and entirely off the market.”

The bomb went off. But instead of pain, inside, she burst with joy.

"I will never stray," said David. "I'll never need to.

You are everything I have ever wanted."

"I believe you," said Jules.

"Jules, you hardly know him," said her sister.

Jules shook her head. She knew this man. She had been waiting for him her whole life. And now, he was here.

"So, that's it?" Romey said. "You're not coming home?"

Jules opened her mouth. And then closed it.

"What about your crops?" asked Romey. "The USDA inspectors are arriving today. They might already be there. This organic certification is what you and Paris have been working so hard for."

It was. And she wanted to see it through. "Paris can handle the inspection. Once we get the certification, he'll calm down. He's never been prone to anger."

As though he'd heard his name called, Paris rounded the corner from the front of the house. Jules didn't see the calm, rational man she'd grown up with. Paris looked red-faced and ready for war.

He was at David's back. David turned, likely from seeing the surprise on Jules's face. Before he could register if the person coming to him was friend or foe, Paris drew his fist and connected it with David's jaw.

# CHAPTER TWENTY-THREE

Porco's head snapped back from the force of something blunt and angry.

For a moment, he'd thought the earlier kiss from Jules had knocked him back on his rear. He wouldn't have put it past the effect of her. He had no clue how he'd kissed other women and thought he'd found any pleasure in the act. Any and all memories of others were quickly fading from his mind until only Jules remained.

And now there were two of her. Not her sister with the short, springy hair. There were two Jules with caramel skin, flashing hazel eyes, and long spirals snaking over him while he lay on the ground.

Why was he on the ground? Had he skipped some time in this long, endless second day of their marriage, and they were now finally getting to enjoy their wedding night properly? But if so, why were there tears in her eyes? Had he hurt her?

No, that couldn't be it. Because he was the one hurting. His eye was throbbing. Now the right eye along with the left eye.

Jules's fingers over his bruised eye was a balm. Behind her, he heard scuffling. More men charged into the picture. He heard the unmistakable grunt of Grizz and the barking orders of Keaton. But all he could focus on was Jules.

"Wow, Porco. The vegan got a drop on you twice?" That was Keaton. Was that censure in his voice or amusement?

Porco sat up with Jules still draped around him. As his vision came into focus, he saw a tall man with a thin build. The guy looked familiar, but Porco couldn't quite place him. Until he saw the man's balled fist. That he remembered well.

"Paris," Jules hissed. "What is the matter with you!"

Porco had seen Jules smiling. He'd seen her frowning. He'd seen her passionate. He'd seen her confused. He'd seen her disappointed. This was the first time he'd seen her angry.

His produce eating, peace-loving, even-toned

wife was a ball of energy. And she was set to launch at the man who'd knocked her husband down. It was taking Grizz and Keaton to hold Paris back from him. Porco got his arms around Jules before she could launch herself at the captive man.

Even with two swollen eyes, this was a battle he had to fight. He'd been prepared to turn the other cheek to Paris after his sucker punch last night. But this was all the zen Porco was going to muster.

"It's all their fault," snarled Paris. "We lost the certification because of them."

Some of the fight to get free went out of Jules at Paris's words. Her hands came to rest on his shoulders. Porco felt his wife's fingers tremble. He turned a murderous glare on Paris. It was one thing to hurt him. He would not stand to have anyone hurt Jules.

But he would have to wait his turn. Brenda stepped between him and Paris.

"You are trespassing on my land," she said. "And you've assaulted one of my residents."

"You assaulted the purity of my lands," said Paris. "The USDA inspector detected pesticides at the boundary between our lands. On our side."

"We stayed away from your land as agreed," said Brenda. "No one sprayed near the border."

A whirring sounded overhead. Up above, soaring through the sky, was a commercial airliner. The timing was uncanny as cold dread washed over Porco. His hands tightened around Jules, certain that if he didn't, she might get away from him.

She tore her gaze from Paris and looked down at him. Concern colored her beautiful face, and she ran a hand over his brow. "David, what's wrong. Are you hurting?"

Porco shook his head, though he felt his insides squeeze. "I did it."

"You couldn't have done anything," she assured him, her heated gaze still on Paris. "None of this is your fault."

Porco swallowed, taking in a deep breath before saying the words that would hurt the woman he loved. Her vanilla scent swirled into his nose. He drunk in her scent, taking in the warm comfort.

"Jules." Her name was a prayer, a balm. He reached for her hands and entwined them with his own.

Jules's concerned melted away. Porco watched as the lines of her forehead creased with something worse than worry. Etched in those lines he saw the markings of dread.

"I was spraying near your lands the other day. I

was using a drone. I lost control and it hovered over your land."

Jules blinked, as though she was seeing the scene play out in her mind. "That was you?"

The fear he'd harbored came true a second later. Jules's fingers shook again. This time, anger wasn't the cause. Despair was, and Porco was at its root.

Porco reached for her again, unwilling to let even a breath of space between them. She didn't snatch her hands from him. She gazed down at their entwined fingers as though she was lost.

"It was an accident," said Porco. "I didn't do it on purpose."

"We lost everything," said Paris. "We won't get the certification. Everything we've worked for all these years, gone because of him."

"I'm sorry, Jules," said Porco. "Tell me how to fix it."

"I don't know," she said, defeat in her tone as she rose. "I've gotta go home and figure this out."

"I'll come with you," said Porco.

He took a step towards her. When their gazes connected, he saw that something had dimmed in her eyes. Her focus shifted from him to her sister, and then to Paris.

"I don't think that's the best idea," Jules said. "I need to work this out with my people."

"With your people?"

"I mean, with my family."

"I'm your family."

Jules sighed. His heart broke on her quiet breath.

"I don't want to start another fight," she said. "Just let me go and take care of this. I'll call you later."

Porco watched as his wife walked off with the man who had been his rival just a day ago. He was gratified to see that Jules turned away from Paris when he motioned her towards his truck. Instead, she hopped into the vehicle with her sister. Before they made a U-turn to head off the property, Jules lifted her gaze and connected with Porco one last time before all he saw was the dust kicked up by the tires.

When the truck was no longer visible from the horizon, he remembered. He'd never given her his cell phone number. And she didn't have one of her own.

## CHAPTER TWENTY-FOUR

It was just a couple of miles down the road, but Jules felt the separation from David acutely. Every yard was a stab in her chest. Every inch was a slow drip of poison in her veins. Dimly she was reminded that a dagger and a vile of poison were how Romeo and Juliet met their ends in the play.

This would not be how the curtain fell on this particular romance. Jules and David weren't two immature kids who made rash decisions.

Well, their marriage within twenty-four hours had been quick, but Jules didn't doubt for a second that they had the stuff to make it last. There was the spark, that ethereal force that told them both they were meant to be. Jules trusted that force more than anything. It was sent from heaven, so it had to be right.

Besides that divine connection, there was so much to recommend her husband that that boy Romeo didn't possess. David was thoughtful and kind. He was loyal and sincere. He was funny and smart. There wasn't a mean, malicious bone in his body.

Paris had struck the large soldier twice, and David hadn't retaliated. The drone had been an accident. She'd seen the plane correct its trajectory with her own eyes.

But the damage was still done.

Romey drove the truck past their house and down into the fields. The border was still many acres away, they would have to walk the rest of the way. The field of beans looked just as sturdy and bountiful as the day before. To the naked eye, nothing was wrong. Only a test could tell that the roots of her land were now tainted.

"You okay?" asked Romey, coming to stand beside her.

Jules opened her mouth, but nothing came out. Her eyes stayed fixed on the horizon. She couldn't see the boundary that ended the commune and began Vance Ranch, but she swore she could feel the dividing line. David had been here just the other day. His actions had caused an even greater rift between their two families.

"That was a stupid question," said Romey. "Of course, you're not okay."

Romey brought Jules into a hug. At first, Jules was shocked. Though the twins had grown up in a loving family, surrounded by an empathic, huggy community, Romey was not prone to physical forms of affection.

"You really care about him?" said Romey. "Don't you?"

Jules couldn't find the words as she snuggled deeper into her sister's embrace. So, she nodded.

"Then we'll figure out how to fix it. It's just a problem, an equation with variables. We just need to do the calculations to find the solution."

Jules wanted to laugh. There was her pragmatic sister. She half believed that Romey would simply solve for X, and the equation would balance itself out.

"The only solution is to sue, to recoup the profit we've lost now that we don't have the certification."

They hadn't even heard Paris approach. Jules

pulled away from Romey to peer at her other lifelong friend. She didn't even recognize the man.

There were lines at the corner of his narrowed eyes where they used to be large and bright. His lips were pinched now. Paris had never been one to grin big and flash his teeth. But he'd always worn a small smile on his face. Dark circles beneath his eyes sat prominently on his high cheeks.

No, he did not look like himself. He looked like his father.

"This is all your husband's fault."

"David said it was a mistake," said Jules. She didn't believe for a second that he would have done this with any malice. For that matter, she didn't think that Brenda would've willfully hurt their prospects.

"It was worse than a mistake," said Paris. "It didn't even occur to him that his actions could be a problem. Those people poisoned our land and our future."

Jules looked around again at her crop. Her beans looked just as healthy as ever. She knew that the chemicals hadn't reached very far, just the small patch at the border. None of the other crops would be affected.

"That's a very dramatic statement," said Romey.

"I'm sure we can explain to the inspector about the mistake. If not, we can at least appeal the decision."

Paris shook his head. "Those chemicals will be out of the land in weeks, but it's another three-year wait for us to try for certification again. All because of one careless action, on one patch of land, on the wrong day of the year."

"Ha!"

They both looked over at Romey. Her eyes were lit like when she had solved one of her puzzles in record time.

"That's it," she said. "The variable."

Romey looked at both Paris and Jules expectantly, as if their brains worked on the same level as hers. They didn't.

"Disown our land," Romey said.

Paris' narrowed gaze widened. His mouth slackened. Gone was the ire that had been a constant on his father's features. He looked horrified, like when one of the children on the commune had gotten injured in the field.

"It makes the most sense," Romey continued. "If our patch of land isn't a part of the commune, then the rest of the crops will get the certification."

"I'm not disowning you." Paris's voice was adamant.

"Why not?"

"You're my family," he said as though it was the most natural thing in the world. And it was.

Gone were the lines at his eyes. He still wasn't smiling, but the pinched look had gone from his mouth. The dark circles under his eyes had brightened as his skin had reddened.

Tears struck Jules's eyes. She ran the three steps it took to get to him. And then she was in her friends' arms.

"There you are," she whispered into his chest. "I've missed you so much."

He stood stiff as a board. He tried wriggling out of her hold, but she would not let him go. Jules held on tighter, not willing to let her second-oldest friend go. Soon, his lean body relaxed. His arms came around her and squeezed her back.

"You're our family too, Paris," she said. "David is also my family."

Once again, Paris stiffened in her hold. But Jules refused to let him go.

"That makes him your family," Jules insisted.

"She's right." Romey came up behind Paris and sandwiched the Montgomery inside a Capulano hug. "Their marriage makes him a member of the commune and part of this community."

"And you know what that means," said Jules. "You have two offenses in the Problem Jar. You're going to have to sit with him in an Empathy Circle."

Paris groaned. But he didn't complain. It was a start, and that's all she needed to begin with.

## CHAPTER TWENTY-FIVE

It had only been an hour, but it felt like an eternity. Porco stood at the boundary line of the two ranches. Here was the scene of the crime, the mistake that could cost him everything.

The fields he'd treated the other day were already showing signs of life. A few seedlings poked their green heads above the cracked earth. Their leaves unfurled as they reached for the sun's rays.

On the other side of the fence, he saw a few beanstalks that stood a might higher than the others that surrounded it. The growth was slight, but the damage was done. The grass was greener, but it was not better.

"How do I fix this?" Porco asked no one in particular.

He was not alone out in the field. Brenda and Keaton had come to survey the ruins. They were leaning against the rail, heads bent in conversation. It was Spinelli who answered Porco.

"It takes three years for lands to become certified organic," said Spinelli. "It's not a quick fix."

Looking out across the field, Porco could feel Jules's presence. She was so close and yet so far. She'd been there every day tending to her beanstalks, and he hadn't known it. Now he had no idea how he'd live another day without her in his arms.

Spinelli came up to his shoulder, his gaze focused on the beanstalks. "We screwed this one up, didn't we?"

"We?"

"The drone wasn't working properly, that was on me."

"I flew it off course."

"I miscalculated." Spinelli looked across the fields. His gaze was hooded with... was that longing?

A squeal brought both their attention round. Bounding towards them was a fat hog. Porco had no idea how the pig moved so fast on those stubby legs.

"Hamlet?"

As if in answer, the pig squealed. It stuck its

snout through the fence. Porco offered the beast his hand, which the pig promptly sniffed and licked.

Wasn't that irony? A pig licking the taste of Porco.

Porco went down to his haunches to scratch the pig's head. Hamlet's snout made it look like it was smiling at him. A soft spot opened in Porco's heart for the pig.

That didn't mean his stomach wouldn't welcome the pig's distant relatives tomorrow morning. Unless it was a requirement for him to bust through this border. Because he knew he would give or give up anything to be with Jules again. Even pork.

In the distance, Porco saw three figures come into view. The first figure he'd recognize anywhere. It was Jules.

The sun took that moment to shine brightly on her face. Time ceased to exist. Distance was no matter. The grass was indeed greener on that side of the fence, and Porco knew that he had to get to the other side.

Shooing the pig aside, he ducked his large body under the fence. Behind him, he heard his friends protest. He paid them no heed. There would be no boundaries in their marriage.

His steps carried him toward Jules. The closer he

got, he saw that she was not alone. She was walking with Paris. She was walking arm in arm with Paris. She was smiling up at Paris with those eyes of light.

Porco's steps faltered. Had he lost her? Was it too late?

Paris stiffened. The man must've seen Porco. There would be another fight. Porco had no more cheeks left to turn. He balled his fingers into a fist.

All the fight went out of Porco as Jules turned her gaze onto him. Her smile blinded him. He could feel the love in her heart even from this distance.

She broke the trance, turning back to Paris. She said something to him. Paris sighed, then he kept moving forward. Jules stayed behind, standing shoulder to shoulder with her sister.

Porco ignored Paris, who was striding towards him. He wanted nothing to do with the man, but he would knock Paris down if he dared keep him from his wife. When Paris was just a yard away, the man opened up his arms.

Porco stopped and put his dukes up.

"It's an Empathy Circle," said Paris.

Porco had no idea what fighting stance the man had taken, but he bounced his toes in preparation.

"I'm sorry," said Paris. "I used my fists instead of my words. I've taken a moment to put myself in your shoes, and I see the error of my ways. With empathy instead of anger in my heart, I offer you a hug to mend the hurt I caused."

Porco looked over his shoulder. Spinelli had come through the fence. Brenda and Keaton remained on their side, but their attention was rapt.

Paris was now in front of him. He had his arms opened wide. He was an easy target.

Porco looked past Paris at his wife. Jules was beaming at him encouragingly. Was this what it would take to win her back? He'd rather give up bacon.

Paris waited patiently. Arms still held open. Tentatively, Porco took a step forward. The embrace was stiff, quick. Porco may have given the man a thump on the back that was harder than necessary.

When they broke apart, Porco received the embrace he'd been hungering for. Jules ran into his arms. He caught her up, pressing her to him. They spun in a circle. When the circle completed, he did not put her down. He was never letting this woman go again.

"So, that's it?" Brenda called. "We're good?"

"We're going to have the commune disown our land," said Romey.

"I haven't agreed to that," said Paris. "Our parents

left this land in trust to us. It's going to take time and lawyers to work any of that out."

"At least that'll get him off my back," Porco heard Brenda mutter behind him.

"That still leaves you without the organic certification," said Spinelli, his gaze sliding towards Romey.

"I know it's not the most elegant solution," said Romey. "But it should take less than three years, which is how long it will take to get another inspector out here."

"Why not just sell this strip of land to me?" said Brenda. "I don't mind the chemicals. Jules has told me that cows like soybean."

But Paris was shaking his head. "We can't sell it to anyone outside of the families of the charter."

"This place and its land regulations," said Keaton, but he said it with a smile. The regulations on land were what caused his hasty marriage with Brenda that turned into lasting love.

Maybe that was it?

"Sell it to me," said Porco.

"Could work" said Romey. "He is family."

Porco liked the sound of that. Gazing down at Jules, he saw that she liked it too. If they owned this land, it would be out from under the thumb of both the Vance ranch and the Verona commune. They would be the buffer between their two worlds, living in their own cocoon of happiness and peace.

And then the dream sank when Paris told him the value of the land. Porco wasn't hurting for cash. But he didn't have that much in his bank account.

"I can cover the rest."

All eyes went to Spinelli. His gaze kept darting to Romey and then looking away with feigned detachment.

"It's partly my fault."

"We run into the same problem," said Paris. "You're not family."

Spinelli's gaze landed on Romey then. He swallowed, his Adam's apple bobbing before he said, "I could become family."

Romey gasped. Her eyes lit, just like her sister's had the first time Porco had seen Jules. He was standing between the two; his best friend and his new sister in law. The pull between them was unmistakable. There were tiny sparks of energy dancing between the two. Even a blind person could see it.

"It's the best solution," Romey finally said, her voice only slightly breathy. "We can get the certification for the rest of the land. Jules can sell her soybeans to the Vances."

"The Keatons," Keaton pipped in, but no one paid him any mind.

"But you'll have to marry him." Paris stuck his thumb out at Spinelli.

"Jordan is intelligent, gainfully employed, and fit," said Romey, ticking each accomplishment off on her fingers. "What more could a woman ask for?"

"Love?" said Jules from inside the cocoon of Porco's arms.

Romey shrugged.

Spinelli mimicked the movement.

"Love is nothing but a construct," said Romey.

"You can't still believe that," said Jules.

"The marriages on the Vance Ranch and the Purple Heart Ranch all started out as marriages of convenience," said Spinelli. "They've all been successful."

"Excellent point," said Romey, tilting her head like Jules did when she was delighted.

"Thank you." Spinelli gave her a grin.

As if they felt the eyes that were definitely on them, they both wiped the grins off their faces and looked away from each other.

Jules opened her mouth to argue the matter

further. Porco turned her, sweeping her back up into his arms so that her feet dangled just below his knees. He pressed his mouth to hers and words failed her.

The spark that had been present between them ignited into a flare. One day the heat they made might dampen into a smolder. Though he doubted it. He was sure it would always be this way between the two of them.

"I missed you," Jules said when he allowed her lips to part from his.

"You never will again," he assured her. "Come on, Hamlet. Let's go home."

The three of them left the others behind to work out the details of the land transfer. He and Jules already done their part. They walked across the acres until they reached the cabin nestled between the two lands who had decided on peace that was now reinforced with love.

Who knew? Maybe someday in the near future, they would even tear the fences down.

# EPILOGUE

"She makes my heart speed up, man. She puts butterflies in my stomach."

Jordan Spinelli rubbed his forefinger over his brow. Porco's words made no logical sense. He supposed it was hyperbole, and not meant to be taken literally. But what else were you supposed to do with words if not take them for their definitive meanings?

If Porco meant that Jules made his heart race, then he could mean that she was engaging his fight or flight responses. In which case, his friend's new wife was either a predator who would eat him alive. Or she was prey that he planned to chase after. Neither seemed an ideal situation to Spinelli's mind.

Then there was the bit about butterflies in the

stomach; an idiomatic phrase. Spinelli had excelled in school, except when it came to the English language and words that had contrasting meanings when put together in different sequences. He didn't understand how an expression that colloquially meant to make one nervous, could be used to describe love.

"That's not love," said Spinelli. "That's a medical condition."

To be honest, he'd never truly understood the meaning of the word love. The dictionary told it was a deep and intense feeling of affection. A secondary definition was that it was interest and pleasure. Spinelli had always found those denotations lacking. Apparently, he wasn't the only one.

Down at the end of the aisle, he saw a woman's shoulders straighten at his words. Her head gave a nod, as though she were in total agreement with him. Porco was still talking, but Spinelli stepped around him, wanting to get a look at the woman who appeared to share his thoughts.

His feet were moving before he had conscious thought to set them in motion. His ears twitched, like a dog's who heard the high pitch of a whistle from its master calling. His fingers tingled, as though the electricity in the room had increased and become a tangible thing. A chill skittered across the back of his neck, even though he'd stepped away from the refrigerated section of the store.

All the while, he kept moving forward. One step, then another. Closer to her, as if drawn.

What was happening to him? Whatever it was, Spinelli wanted to understand the phenomenon. To study it and pick it apart.

His eyes were glued to the woman, whose back was still turned to him. All he could see of her was her hair. Short spirals of black, bronze, and gold radiated from the crown of her head. As though she was a ball of burning gas and her hair was the radiation it gave off.

As though she sensed him coming near, she turned, and Spinelli stopped in his tracks.

His heart rate sped up. His stomach muscles fluttered. His palms dampened. Was he having a medical condition of his own?

Then her gaze found his. Intelligence shone brightly in her hazel eyes. In the slight smile she offered him, Spinelli felt understood, even though he didn't know this girl. He felt seen, even though this was the first time he'd laid eyes on her. For some reason, she looked familiar to him. But his brain was short-circuiting and he couldn't place her.

They stared at one another. Spinelli spoke six languages. At the moment, he couldn't remember a greeting in any of them.

"Hello," she said.

Spinelli snapped his fingers. That was the word. He repeated it back to her.

And then they stared some more.

She squinted at him as though he was a problem. He could see her mind trying to work him out. Her astute gaze took in his body, taking her time as her eyes roamed over the muscles stretching his shirt. He wanted her eyes back on his face so that she could see that he was smart too.

"You're right," she said finally.

"I am?"

"It is a medical condition."

"What I'm feeling?" The racing pulse. The sweat on his brow. The thrumming in his ears of a single word on repeat. The word sounding like mine.

"Love," she clarified, looking past him. "It's a medical condition. One that my sister's new husband seems to suffer from quite a lot."

Spinelli followed her gaze. Porco was where he'd left him, but his friend was no longer alone. A woman trailed a finger down his chest and Porco looked to be doing nothing to stop it.

"I tried to tell her that there's no such thing as true love."

Spinelli turned back to the woman who he now deduced was Jules' twin sister. How had he not seen that before? Maybe because they looked nothing alike. Romey Capulano didn't have that same starry-eyed look as her sister. There was a sparkle in Romey's gaze that Spinelli could only quantify as brilliant.

"I need to find her and put an end to this marriage." Romey turned on her heel and stormed out.

With a glance at his friend, Spinelli hurried out the door to follow Romey. Like a magnet, he was on her heels, attaching himself to her side. "I'll come with you. I know where she is."

*I don't know about you,*
*but I think what just happened might be love at first sight between Jordan and Romey.*
*But these two are going to deny it until there's no other solution before them.*
*Forget the science and fall in love with*
*The Rancher takes his Love at First Sight.*

## ALSO BY SHANAE JOHNSON

Shanae Johnson was raised by Saturday Morning cartoons and After School Specials. She still doesn't understand why there isn't a life lesson that ties the issues of the day together just before bedtime. While she's still waiting for the meaning of it all, she writes stories to try and figure it all out. Her books are wholesome and sweet, but her are heroes are hot and heroines are full of sass!

And by the way, the E elongates the A. So it's pronounced Shan-aaaaaaaa. Perfect for a hero to call out across the moors, or up to a balcony, or to blare outside her window on a boombox. If you hear him calling her name, please send him her way!

**You can sign up for Shanae's Reader Group at**

**http://bit.ly/ShanaeJohnsonReaders**

**Also By Shanae Johnson**

**The Rangers of Purple Heart**

*The Rancher takes his Convenient Bride*

*The Rancher takes his Best Friend's Sister*

*The Rancher takes his Runaway Bride*

*The Rancher takes his Star Crossed Love*

*The Rancher takes his Love at First Sight*

*The Rancher takes his Last Chance at Love*

**The Brides of Purple Heart**

*On His Bended Knee*

*Hand Over His Heart*

*Offering His Arm*

*His Permanent Scar*

*Having His Back*

*In Over His Head*

*Always On His Mind*

*Every Step He Takes*

*In His Good Hands*

*Light Up His Life*

*Strength to Stand*

**The Rebel Royals series**

*The King and the Kindergarten Teacher*

*The Prince and the Pie Maker*

*The Duke and the DJ*

*The Marquis and the Magician's Assistant*

*The Princess and the Principal*